A LITTLE
NIGHT RAINBOW

A LITTLE NIGHT RAINBOW

•

SUSAN AYLWORTH

AVALON BOOKS
THOMAS BOUREGY AND COMPANY, INC.
401 LAFAYETTE STREET
NEW YORK, NEW YORK 10003

C. 1

PRINTED IN THE UNITED STATES OF AMERICA
ON ACID-FREE PAPER
BY HADDON CRAFTSMEN, BLOOMSBURG, PENNSYLVANIA

For Jared and Stephanie.
For Tanis Jason,
with love.

And always,
for Roger

Prologue

It was only April, not even Easter yet, but a strong Santa Ana wind was blowing a heat wave into the L.A. basin. Residents were running for cover, turning on air conditioners and hiding indoors. But in the factories of Carmody Auto Parts, in an industrial area of Tustin, California, the temperature was always a perfect seventy-six degrees, the humidity always delicately balanced. In fact, everything in the plant worked perfectly. The boss insisted on it.

Buzzers buzzed on schedule, whirring things whirred, and the conveyor belts along the assembly lines kept up a pleasing pace as they turned out specimen after specimen of "the best replacement parts your auto dollar can buy." Yet for Maxwell Simon Carmody—founder, owner, president, and C.E.O. of it all—the sight failed to bring the usual jolt of humble satisfaction.

"Mozart. I need Mozart," Max murmured aloud, then slumped into his office, still holding the certified letter that had just turned his world upside down. He passed his highly efficient secretary-caretaker, Lena, who asked, "You okay, Max?" as he went by, mumbled something unintelligible that he hoped would put her off for a while, then shut the door as he entered his domain. Though he believed in an open-door approach to management, and usually practiced it with diligence, today he needed the privacy that the solid door could offer. Today he needed peace.

Rifling through a stack of CDs, he settled on "Eine Kleine Nachtmusik" and put it on to play, letting the first dramatic chords catch his emotions. *Good*, he thought. *Good. I can use "A Little Night Music."* Settling into his chair, his hand over his eyes, he let the music's peace wash over him.

Max sighed. Mozart had always had this effect on him. In fact, he was a fan of all the great composers of the classical period—Mozart, Haydn, the whole bunch; had been ever since he was a kid. That was one good thing his mother had done for him, anyway.

He thought of his mother now as he held his ex-wife's letter in his hand. *We aren't much good at marrying, are we, Mom?* he thought with self-deprecating humor. He had often joked that marriages ran in his family, until they ran out.

He'd almost lost track of how many marriages his parents and stepparents had accumulated by now. He himself was the product of his mother's second marriage, the intense but short-lived union with banker-financier Simon Carmody. She had been married before, and had borne a half brother who had lived and died before Max ever had time to meet him. Then there was a lull in her life before she had married Simon, followed by the two short years necessary to produce him before his parents had separated. He had been four when his mother had married "Daddy Taylor," then just short of six when his half sister, Margaret, was born, and twelve when that third marriage ended, leaving him the oldest child and only son of a single mom.

By the time his mother's fourth husband had entered their lives, he was graduating high school and pretty much on his own. It had been Mom and Meg who had moved to Rainbow Rock, Arizona, where his mother's newest husband was the high school principal. He still found it highly ironic that after years of escape in southern California, Meg had chosen to go back to Rainbow Rock to live.

Meanwhile his mother had married once more—and had been single for a while since the conclusion of that debacle. His father, whom he had seen on occasional holidays and for one obligatory week every summer until he had turned eighteen and put a stop to that, had been through three more wives and a series of look-alike girlfriends, each of whom seemed interchangeable with any of the others, like the brake parts and transmission systems his company built. That alone made an impressive list of marriages, without even counting those the come-and-go stepparents had contracted.

I don't know why I ever imagined I could marry in the first place, he thought, looking again at Joanna's letter. Maybe it was only because Joanna had been so beautiful, so exciting and full of life, that he had even hoped to try. *And because I was too young to see how little aptitude I had for family living*, he recalled, remembering the fragile hope of that long-ago time. But it did little good to ponder that now.

The fact was, he had made that mistake, marrying Joanna when he was twenty-four and still finishing his college degree in mechanical engineering, then putting her, and eventually their child, on the back burner while he designed a better braking system, a more trouble-free transmission— and used some emotional blackmail to get his wealthy father to stake him the seed money that had eventually grown into Carmody Auto Parts. While struggling to get the company going, he kept meaning to spend more time with his family, but it just never happened. Like his parents before him, he had built a business and neglected his family until he had no family left.

Oh, he had done the obligatory daddy thing for the kid, just as his father had done for him—two weeks every summer, usually with a hired nanny, occasional weekends and holidays, and a great secretary who never failed to pick just the right gift for every Christmas and birthday, and to see that it got mailed on time. But take over full-time care? He shook his head as he looked again at the letter. Joanna had to be out of her mind.

"You have to admit it's fair," Joanna said, her voice frightfully calm, when Max talked with her half an hour later. "I've raised her for the last twelve, almost thirteen years."

"And you've done a great job," Max answered, realizing as he said it that he hadn't seen enough of their daughter to know whether Joanna was doing a great job or not. "Which is why I don't understand why you want me to take over at this point."

Joanna sighed, and he remembered for a moment how lovely she could be when she adopted that winsome look and tossed her soft, honey-gold hair. A woman like Joanna deserved better than he'd given her. He was glad she had married again. "Oh, Max," she said, "don't you see that I need a break here? And you don't know what Marcie is like now that she's almost a teenager. I swear—you put your kid to bed one night and she's a perfectly normal child, a rather likable human being. Then bam! She wakes up a sneering, growling slug and you know she's almost thirteen."

"But Jo—"

"Besides," Joanna cut in, and there was more pressure behind her voice now. "She and Carl don't get along at all, haven't from the first, and I think she's jealous of little Teddy. She needs to feel special, especially in her father's eyes. No, Max, I'm not going to be talked out of this one. Marcella is coming to stay with you.''

"But how am I going to—"

"I don't know, Max. Figure something out. It's only for the summer, and frankly, it's about time."

"Yes, I know, but—"

"She'll be there the day after school's out. That's June sixth," Joanna responded firmly, and the line went dead. The dial tone told Max he had better start figuring fast. June sixth was only six weeks away.

Whether it was inspiration or sheer desperation that brought Meg's face to mind, Max didn't know, but in that moment he suddenly thought of the one person in the family who seemed to have a little talent for domesticity.

His half sister had gone back to Rainbow Rock some six years earlier and had married an old high school chum. Of course, he had been in merger negotiations during the week of their wedding. . . .

He smiled as he thought of it; his business had grown dramatically as a result of that deal. Though that obviously meant he hadn't attended the ceremony, he'd had an opportunity to see Meg and Jim once since then, at a family thing one of their aunts had cooked up when their mother's mother had turned seventy-five. Meg had seemed happy and her husband—it *was* Jim, wasn't it?—seemed to be successful enough, even if he was a little eccentric with that Schwarzenegger build and all that long, blond hair. Then he'd received a birth announcement when their child—Aileen, was it? Allison? Alexander?—was born. Maybe Meg would take Marcie for the summer. He could always hope.

Feeling just a little like the heel he probably was, he pushed the button on the intercom and asked Lena to look up his sister's married name—darn! why couldn't he remember that?—and get a listing for her home in Arizona. A few minutes later, he was on the phone to Meg.

"So you see, I'm in something of a spot here," Max said, concluding his story, and thinking he'd done rather well. He had been careful to ask after Meg's health and to ask about Jim and the baby (a daughter—her name was Alexis; he'd made a note) before explaining his situation. He'd gone for family warmth and an appeal to the maternal side of his half sister. He hoped he'd built his case well. "Marcie needs a place to stay for the summer, and well, it's out of the question for me to stay home with her. I was hoping—"

"You were hoping I'd pick up the pieces and take care of your daughter for you," Meg said, and Max could tell from her tone that the scenario wasn't playing out as he'd planned.

"She could probably help you out a lot," Max went on, giving his prepared sales pitch. "She's almost thirteen. She could—"

"Maybe she could and maybe she couldn't," Meg said, her voice more gentle now, "but I think that's quite beside the point, don't you, Max?"

He hesitated. "I—I don't . . ."

"Seems to me it's about time you got to know your daughter, and you're not going to do that if you dump her in Rainbow Rock for the summer. Say, hang on a minute. I just thought of something."

He was about to interrupt her, to try to find some way of getting her to come around—begging, if that's what it took, or bribery, even—but she had covered the phone with her hand and he could hear muffled bits of conversation in the background that said she was talking to someone. Then Meg came on again.

"Here's what I will do for you," she said, in the tone

of a seasoned business negotiator. "Jim just came in and he and I had a brief chat about your situation. We have a big house here, Max, and even with Alexis, there are still two empty bedrooms and an extra bath. We won't take Marcella for you, but if you and Marcie want to come together, there's space here for both of you for as long as you like."

"Together? Meg, that's out of the question! How can I get away from my business? I've never been away for as much as a week, let alone a whole summer. How—"

"Then it's time you did. Tell everyone you're going on vacation."

"But I—"

"It's all or nothing, Max," Meg said, and Max let the thought pass that he admired the steel in both the women he'd talked to today. "Either you come and bring Marcie with you, or you're on your own for the summer."

"But I can't—"

"Let me know what you decide," Meg said, and he could tell she was hanging up.

"Meg!" he called in a panic.

"Yes, Max?"

"Meg, I can't . . ." But it was pointless to argue. Max sighed. "I'll see what I can do."

"Thatta boy." He could hear the smugness in her voice. "Just let us know when you're coming."

"I'll get back to you," he answered weakly, and put the phone in its cradle.

Max Carmody sat alone in his office, unable to remember when he had felt so trapped. Not even Mozart was calming him now, and it didn't help that he suspected the women in his life were right—that it really was time he got to know his daughter. Besides, he could remember bragging to a business colleague just last week that his business was set up so efficiently, it could practically run itself.

That was largely the work of his production manager, Nathan Bailey, the straw boss of his outfit who made everything run. Max liked to be a hands-on manager, up close and personal, but he knew he didn't always have to be, not with someone as competent as Nate around. Whether he liked the idea or not, with Nate in charge, Carmody Auto Parts could probably get by without him—for a little while, anyway.

"Lena," he called, punching the button on the intercom again. "Call all my managers in here, will you? Looks like we need an impromptu meeting."

"Sure, Max," she answered. Good secretary that she was, she was keeping the questions to herself, though he could hear the curiosity in her voice.

"And you come in, too, Lena. Send in Nate first, then bring a notepad and come in with the rest of the management crew in, say, fifteen minutes?"

"You've got it, Max," she answered, and for the umpteenth hundredth time, he blessed her efficiency.

He cut off the intercom and tapped the fateful letter on his desk. Though he didn't doubt he could come up with another solution—a nanny for the summer, maybe, or a special-talents summer camp to buy the kid off—he was beginning to believe his family responsibilities deserved a little of what he had to give them. "Looks like I'm going to Rainbow Rock," he mumbled, and found there was actually some pleasure in the thought.

Chapter One

It was May twenty-ninth, almost summer, yet the blue-gray thunderheads that towered above the high plateaus of the Little Colorado River basin warned of a winter storm. *Looks like it might snow*, Cretia thought as she entered the offices of Rainbow Productions, the independent video company that had become her second home. The thought was not the least unsettling. It had snowed on the night she graduated high school some thirteen years before—the only graduate to go through ceremonies with a husband and three-month-old daughter in the audience. There was often a maverick storm late in the year before summer settled in.

Cretia unlocked the front door, put the OPEN sign out, and turned on the heater-cooler system. The wall thermometer showed fifty-eight degrees—good for their stock of videos, but a bit chilly for working. She hung her jacket on the coat tree, but kept her sweater until the office warmed up. Then she went to the CD player, lifted off the stack of classical albums she had selected for background music, and put on a disc of Sousa marches. The band opened with "The Stars and Stripes Forever" and Cretia hummed along, turning up the volume as she prepared her work space for the day.

It was only the end of May, still weeks away from the Fourth of July, but Lucretia Gina Vanetti Sherwood was celebrating Independence Day.

Seven years ago today she had declared *enough* and had left her troubled marriage, taking Lydia and Danny Junior with her—filled with trepidation, but believing her choice was best for them all. Until then she had believed she could make her marriage work, if she only tried hard enough. Or at least, she had been too fearful to dare braving it as a single mother to leave. Until then Danny Sherwood, even in his drunken periods, had been rough only with her, but that evening in late May seven years ago, when he had threatened her children, Cretia knew she had to leave. She had thrown a few things into boxes, then into the rear of their old hatchback, carried the sleeping children out to their car seats, and headed for a cheap motel in Holbrook, a few miles away.

That had been only the beginning of her struggle, for she had no work skills and little confidence in her own abilities, and Danny had made things as difficult as possible. Still she had gone through with her plans and, whenever she weakened, had remembered the fear in her babies' faces. By sheer coincidence, it had been exactly one year later, on May twenty-ninth, six years ago, that she had finally received her divorce decree.

And she was a different person now—healthier and stronger than she could have imagined six years before. *Prettier, too,* she thought as she caught a glimpse of her reflection in the office window. Oh, she'd been attractive enough as a kid—the only freshman girl to catch the interest of one of the senior football jocks. After that, she and Danny had dated sporadically until late in her junior year when they'd made the trip into southern Nevada with some fake I.D. that claimed she was already eighteen. After that, she'd gone downhill fast.

Lydia's birth during Cretia's senior year and the struggle to finish high school with a baby and little help at home had taken an early toll, followed by some serious "comfort eating" during her difficult marriage, and a long period of little or no money when she didn't dare spend for a new blouse or a haircut, or even a tube of lipstick. It had been a tough road to rebuild enough confidence in herself to believe she *could* look good. The job at Rainbow Productions had been the key to that, and she thanked her employers daily for believing in her enough to give her that chance.

Kurt McAllister and his sister-in-law, Meg, had created Rainbow Productions out of a few dollars, a good combination of knowledge and skills, and a dream. Then a little more than two years ago, they had trusted Cretia enough to give her a key to the front door and a job as receptionist. Since then, Meg had borne her first child; Alexa Babbidge, now Kurt's wife, had come to work as a part-time scriptwriter; and Cretia had developed additional skills besides just answering phones and filling orders. Now Meg was training her as a field producer.

Imagine! she thought as she jotted down the recorded messages that had come in from the East Coast during the early hours. *Little no-account Lucretia Sherwood is going to be a video producer!* It certainly beat the odds, and it beat to death all the fearsome prophecies Danny Sherwood had pronounced upon her when she had finally built up the courage to leave. *No question about it. Rainbow Productions has been a miracle for me*, she thought, feeling greater confidence than ever in her talents, abilities—even her looks. In time to the music, she marched across the office to the stockroom, thinking, *Look out, world! I'm ready for anything!*

As if on cue, the back door opened and Meg McAllister stepped in with her daughter in a shoulder-pack. " 'Morning,'' she called. ''What's with the marches?''

''Sousa,'' Cretia called over the trombone section. ''Independence Day.''

Meg nodded knowingly. ''That's right,'' she shouted. ''I'd forgotten. Happy Independence Day.'' Then she wrinkled her brow. ''Now that we've done that, do you think we can have something quieter? I can barely hear my own thoughts—not that they're all that interesting.''

''No problem.'' Cretia grinned and replaced the Sousa marches with the classical CDs she usually favored, simultaneously decreasing the volume. A lovely concerto for viola and flute began.

Meg took a deep, cleansing breath. ''Ah! Now that's more like it. Mozart, right?''

''You know me,'' Cretia answered.

''I like Mozart, too,'' Meg said. ''He was a favorite of my mother's during my younger years.'' She set Alexis in the corner playpen and spun the dial on the Play Center in its corner, hoping to distract her child. ''We listened to a lot of Mozart when I was young.'' Then to the baby, she murmured, ''There now, sweetheart. Settle down and entertain yourself so Mommy can get some work done.''

''There's a nice, almost predictable kind of order to the compositions of the classical period,'' Cretia observed as she loaded the computer disk that contained their template for invoices. ''The rhythms are stable and solid and most of the pieces play out elegant variations on the theme they set in the beginning.''

''Unlike music of the Romantic period,'' Meg chimed in. ''It's full of surprises.''

''Or Baroque,'' Cretia answered. ''All those syncopated rhythms.'' It pleased her to be able to talk about this, or anything, and have her companion treat her like she knew something. She'd gone as long without that kind of respect as she had without a trip to the beauty parlor.

Meg settled at her desk and pulled out a few files. Cretia started creating invoices for the morning's newest video orders. Alexis made soft little humming sounds while she played in the corner. For a time, they worked quietly, each absorbed in her own tasks. Then Cretia spoke to Meg. "I thought you weren't scheduled to come in until later."

"I wasn't, but I got to thinking about the request we had last week from that university in Virginia, the ones who wanted to know if we had a follow-up on *The Weaver's Way*?"

Cretia nodded. *The Weaver's Way*, a documentary piece on Navajo weaving, had been the first project Kurt and Alexa had developed together, and their hottest-selling product, recognized in Hollywood as "best documentary of the year." She took requests and orders for it constantly. "So?" she prompted.

"So it occurred to me that we *could* do a follow-up, a sequel of sorts."

Cretia turned to look at Meg, who began talking animatedly. "We could do interviews with some of the weavers who've made the transition from traditional weaving into recognition as serious players in the art world."

"Like the woman whose rug auctioned for a half-million at Sotheby's?"

"Yeah," Meg answered, "like her. Jim represents most of them, so I have an easy entrée into that arena," she said, speaking of her husband's work as a dealer in Native American art. "I think it would be interesting to look at the tension between the everyday lives of these women who still live in hogans and herd their own sheep, and the upscale world where their work sells."

"Sounds like a winner to me," Cretia answered, then shrugged as she added, "but then, what do I know?"

"A lot," Meg said with conviction. "Don't sell yourself short, Cretia. You have good instincts, and you're turning into a fine field producer. In fact, I'll be talking with Kurt about this new weaving project over the next few days. If we decide to go with it, I may turn it over to you—at least as far as the fieldwork is concerned."

Cretia felt her heart rate pick up. "Are you serious?"

"Never more so," Meg responded. "Most of the location stuff will be shot on the reservation, and I don't want to take Alexis tooling around out there, or leave her for long periods while I'm on the road. Do you think you could work things out with Lydia and Danny?"

"Sure. At least I think so. There wouldn't be any overnights involved, would there?"

"Maybe a few, for the weavers on the New Mexico side, or over by Tuba City. But I expect most of the reservation shooting would just be long days."

"I can do it," Cretia answered with more conviction than she felt. "Lydia is thirteen now and I've put her in charge at home for my normal days in the office. She *loves* lording it over Danny."

Meg grinned. "I'm sure she does."

"If I have a backup for emergencies when I'm out of town, the kids ought to be able to handle things pretty well, and I think my mother will take them during overnight trips, if there aren't too many."

"Then it sounds like we're set." Meg turned back to her work, but a moment later, she asked, "Cretia?"

"Um?"

"You did just say Lydia is thirteen now, didn't you?"

"Um-hm. Why?"

"You just gave me an idea," Meg answered. "My niece is coming to stay for the summer—"

"You're taking her for the whole summer?"

"Not exactly. I told Max I'd only take her if he came, too."

"Who's Max?" Cretia asked.

"My brother. Well, half brother really."

Cretia felt her jaw drop. "I—I didn't know you had a brother."

"Like I said, he's a half brother, and six years older, so he was out of the house by the time I started eighth grade. Still, he's about the only family I have and he just found out he has to take care of his daughter, Marcella, for the summer. His ex-wife thought it was time he took some of the responsibility for a change, and I thought it was time he got to know Marcie a little. She's almost thirteen and, apparently, she's really feeling it."

"I know what you mean there," Cretia observed with a knowing nod. "I sometimes have to remind Lydia that *I'm* the mother in our house. Danny keeps telling her she's breaking the One-Mommy-Per-Person Rule."

"I hope that's the only rule Marcie is breaking," Meg murmured, her voice so low Cretia barely heard her. "Anyway, I told Max I wouldn't take Marcie unless he came, too."

"He can get away from his job that long?"

Meg shrugged. "He owns the company, so I guess he can get away whenever he wants—assuming he can stay in touch."

"With phone, fax, and FedEx, anybody can work anywhere."

"Almost," Meg responded. "Except maybe for video producers. We kind of have to go where the pictures are."

Cretia agreed, then paused for a moment before asking, "When are they coming? Your brother and niece, I mean."

"They'll be here the end of next week," Meg said, "or the beginning of the week after, depending on how fast Max makes the trip from L.A. Marcie's going to be lonesome without her friends. Assuming she's not too bad an influence, do you think she and Lydia can hang out together? At least now and then?''

Cretia smiled. ''I'm relieved. I thought maybe you were going to ask me to take her for the summer.''

Meg chuckled. ''Now there's a thought.''

''But seriously, folks,'' Cretia joked, cutting in. ''Honestly, Meg, I think Lydia would love having another girl to pal around with. She doesn't see her school friends much in the summertime, either, and she'd probably get a big kick out of catching up on the L.A. fashion trends.''

''We'll count on it, then. I'll let you know as soon as they arrive.''

They both resumed their work, but it was less than a minute before Alexis pinched her finger by pushing the Play Center against the corner of the playpen. She began to wail inconsolably, calling, ''Mama! Mama, up!'' until Meg lifted her in her arms. Putting the offended finger in her mouth, she laid her head against her mother's shoulder, still wailing, though it seemed to be more for effect now that she had the comfort she wanted.

''I think I've found all the files I'll need,'' Meg said. ''I'm going to take Allie home now. By the time this crying jag has worn off, she'll probably be ready for her morning nap. Then I can put her down while I write up my ideas for Kurt to review.''

''Sounds good,'' Cretia answered. ''See you later, then.''

''Right,'' Meg said, ''and Cretia? I'll let you know when Marcie gets into town. Thanks again for agreeing to let Lydia hang out with her. Oh, and do let me know if she turns out to be a problem.''

Cretia responded with a confident smile. ''I don't think there'll be any problems. Lydia's pretty tough.''

''Like her mother,'' Meg said, and Cretia warmed with pride. ''See you later.''

"See you," Cretia answered as Meg and Alexis went out the back. She saw Meg pass the stockroom and a sliver of déjà vu popped into her mind. Hadn't she just been standing there a few minutes ago, telling the world she could handle anything? She shivered, and not just from the cold. Some sixth sense was shouting that Meg's niece, Marcie, might just be the answer to her challenge.

Blocking out the incessant nagging from the other side of the front seat, Max checked his watch and shook his head in disbelief. Nine hours. He'd been with Marcie for all of *nine hours*, and already he was beginning to wonder if he'd survive the next nine weeks.

"Look, Daddy! Fort Apache. They've got real Indian stuff! Can we stop, Daddy? Daddy, please?"

"No, Marcie." He was doing his best to keep his tone civil.

"But they've got cherry cider. Doesn't that sound good, Daddy? Cherry cider? And you can buy me that Indian bracelet you promised—"

"I promised?" That one almost got his goat. "Marcella Carmody, I promised no such thing."

"But you said—"

"Stop it, Marcie." And this time there was an edge to his tone. "We're almost there."

"You've been saying that for *miles*."

"It's true nevertheless. So you can quit nagging, because we're not stopping again until we get to your Aunt Meg's house. Do you understand me?"

"Yeah, yeah." Marcie put on an exaggerated pout and flopped her head against the back of the seat, arms folded across her chest.

Max was grateful he'd never been the temperamental sort. He warned himself to remember that. Marcie was going to test the full reserve of his patience—and then some.

In spite of his pronouncement, they hadn't gone five miles before she was at it again. "Kachina Trading Post! Look, Daddy! They have a real live jackelope!"

"I don't think so, Marcie. There's no such thing as a jackelope."

"There is. I've seen pictures. Come on, Daddy. Let's stop. Please?"

"Marcella, I told you we're not stopping again." Max accelerated past the off-ramp to the Kachina Trading Post just to emphasize his point. As he did so, he asked himself what had made his daughter think he was made of money.

Almost as quickly, he realized the answer: *he* had. Until this morning when he picked her up at her mother's home in Buena Park, he had been little more to Marcie than a provider of gifts and treats and an occasional trip to a theme park, zoo, or beach. He winced as he realized it might take some effort to persuade Marcella that he was something other than Santa Claus in disguise. He'd spent too many years teaching her that that was exactly what he was. He sighed. She was going to use up all the patience he could muster.

"Daddy, Daddy," she started in again as they left the freeway in Holbrook and turned north toward Rainbow Rock.

"Marcella, I told you we are not going to stop again," Max said firmly, then broke his word within minutes when he couldn't follow Meg's final directions and had to stop at an ersatz "trading post" to make a phone call. He took a minute to call Nate while he was at it. Though he'd only been away from the business a few hours, and today wasn't even a normal workday, he still needed to check in at the factory, just to be sure everything was all right.

By the time he got back to the car, Marcie had prepared a lengthy speech about how unfair he was being. Max sighed and wiped perspiration from his brow as he turned the car in the direction of his sister's home. It was going to be a long, hot summer.

"Rotten pile of junk!" Cretia kicked the right front tire just to let the car know what she thought of its latest stunt, leaving her stranded on the side of the road with two hungry kids. Predictably, she accomplished nothing but hurting her toes.

"I don't think that's going to help, Mother," Lydia intoned from the front passenger seat.

Reminding herself the car problems were not her daughter's fault, Cretia tried to keep the sarcasm out of her voice as she answered, "You're right, dear."

She popped the hood release and went around the front to prop it open. Seconds later, her son joined her. "Maybe I can help?"

Cretia sighed. "I don't know, honey. Maybe you can. I sure can't figure out what's going on. It's almost like it's running too rich—like it flooded itself out while running down the highway." She paused, rubbing her chin in frustration. "I don't even know if that's possible."

"Sounds like it's probably the carburetor," Danny said importantly.

Cretia nodded. "I expect you're right, but I haven't a clue what to do about it."

"I'll bet Dad could fix it."

Cretia bit her lip rather than telling her son how she would feel about asking for help from his father. "I'll bet he could," she answered.

Lydia joined them then, just as a car passed, then pulled onto the right side of the highway and backed up, coming toward them. "Maybe the cavalry is coming to the rescue?" Lydia asked.

"Could be," Cretia answered. "I could use the guys in white hats about now."

"Aw, Mom," Danny whined. "You know the cavalry guys wore blue hats."

"I don't care what color his hat is if he knows what to do with this carburetor," Cretia responded, then turned gratefully to meet her would-be rescuer.

"I thought you said we weren't going to stop," Marcie nagged as Max pulled to the roadside and began backing up.

"I didn't intend to, Marcie, but I can't leave a woman stranded alone on the highway with a couple of kids—not if there's anything I can do to help."

"How do you know they're not carjackers?"

"For heaven's sake, Marcie. How do they know *we're* not carjackers? Haven't you ever helped somebody out just 'cause it's the right thing to do?"

"Are you kidding? In L.A.?"

"I stand corrected," Max said, reminding himself he was talking to his thirteen-year-old daughter. "Don't ever pull over to help anybody on the roads in L.A. If somebody needs help, use your cell phone and tell the cops."

"So how come you can stop for somebody? And how come it's okay here? Is this another one of your confused double standards, Dad? Because if it is—"

"Marcella!" He put enough power into it that Marcie stopped in mid-whine. Max set the emergency brake, then moderated his tone. "I'm going to go see if I can help. You can stay in the car if you prefer, or you can come and talk to the kids. The girl there looks about your age." He slid his tool kit out from under the driver's seat and opened the door.

"Whatever, Dad." Marcie didn't bother to hide her sarcasm, but she got out of the car and followed behind Max as he approached the woman.

"What seems to be the trouble?" he asked as he neared her.

"We think it may be the carburetor," the woman answered, turning toward the engine as she spoke. It was a smooth, natural, unselfconscious motion, and utterly feminine. Max, who until now had seen only a woman in need of help, was instantly aware of how attractive she was.

"Uh, maybe I can have a look," he said, giving a nod to the boy who hovered protectively at his mother's side. He stepped in beside the woman and was struck by the scent of her—rich, like honeysuckle and orange blossoms on a summer afternoon.

"I sure appreciate you stopping," the woman said. She turned slightly toward him as she spoke, and her long, dark hair brushed his bare arm just below his shirtsleeve. His mouth went dry.

"Uh, no problem," he said, feeling as tongue-tied as a kid at a school dance. He struggled to remember that his daughter was behind him, striking up a conversation with the other girl. If he didn't want to embarrass her, as well as himself, he'd better get his concentration centered on that carburetor—and fast. He leaned in closer, breathing deeply of hot engine smells.

"It seems to be running rich," the woman said. Her voice was as warm and rich as her scent. Max thought he could get lost in it.

"Um, uh, yeah. I'll check that," he said, opening the carburetor.

For the next few minutes, Max fought to focus his attention on the task at hand. He couldn't remember when he'd ever been so instantly, intensely attracted to anyone. Every move she made distracted him; every word she spoke rang through him. It was only through long experience with more engines than he could count that he was able to spot the trouble and make the necessary adjustment.

"There, see if you can start 'er up," he said as he finished, not quite daring to meet the woman's eyes. They were brown eyes, as rich as dark, sweet chocolate, and huge in her perfect oval face. *Max, get a grip*, he chided himself as the engine turned over. *You're losing it, man.*

"You did it !" the woman called as she joined him again. "I really can't thank you enough. Can I pay you for your trouble?" She was reaching for her wallet.

"Heavens, no!" Max couldn't imagine taking money for these few minutes of pure delight. Heck, he ought to be paying her for letting him stand next to her, breathe her fragrance, touch her hair. "It's a temporary fix, anyway. You'll have to get it in for service soon."

"I'll do that," she said, then, "Lydia, Danny, we're going now."

"Okay," the boy answered. "Come on, Sis."

"Yeah, yeah," the girl responded, and it was only then that Max noticed how thick the two teens had become in such a short time. Marcie hadn't whined in at least eight minutes.

"Oh, maybe you can return the favor," he said to the woman as he closed the hood. He took his last jotted directions from his shirt pocket. "I'm supposed to turn right on Hummingbird Lane. Can you tell me how far ahead that is?"

"You passed it," the woman answered in that liquid honey voice. She turned and pointed, and again he was struck by the easy way she moved. He also made a point of noticing her left hand—bare of jewelry, not even a wedding ring. "It'll be the second turn on your left as you go back."

"Thanks," he said.

"Oh, no. Thank you," the woman answered, beaming a megawatt smile, and Max thought he might melt right on the spot.

"No problem," he murmured, then stepped out of the way as the little family loaded into the car. The woman waved as she pulled away and Max followed her with his eyes until she had passed his car.

"She's really nice, Daddy," Marcie began.

"Uh-huh," Max responded, thinking it odd that she had noticed, then tuning her out as he fell into step beside her, walking back toward their car.

"Her name's Lydia and she lives here. She gave me her address and phone. She said maybe we could get together later. What do you think, Dad? Don't you think that would be okay?"

"Huh? Oh yeah, uh-huh," Max answered without really hearing. He was thinking what a shame it was that he hadn't even gotten the woman's name, or asked for her phone number.

By the time they finally pulled up in front of Meg's home in the hills outside of Rainbow Rock, Max was feeling fairly optimistic about spending the next nine weeks in Arizona. Even Marcie's mood had improved. She'd been babbling nonstop ever since they had left the little family by the roadside, and she hadn't nagged once in at least twenty minutes.

"There you are!" Meg called as she came out the front door that seemed to be set in living rock, a baby on her hip. "We were about ready to send out a search party."

"Yeah, well," Max grumbled good-naturedly. "I drove up this way twice and turned back because I couldn't see a house."

"Oops!" Meg said. "I probably should have warned you about that." She turned to Marcie, holding out a hand. "You must be Marcella. Welcome to Rainbow Rock."

Marcie drifted past Meg's outstretched hand, inspecting

the front door with wide eyes. "You guys live in a mountain?"

"Marcie, remember your manners!" Max said.

Meg smiled and stepped next to her niece, putting her free arm around the girl's waist. "In a way, we do," she answered. "My husband Jim designed the place to take advantage of the natural setting. Would you like to see it?"

Marcie's expression brightened. "Yeah. Sure."

It was Meg who turned to Max and added, "If that's okay with you, Dad."

"Sure," he said. He watched as Meg and Marcie disappeared into the wall of rock, then decided the luggage could wait and followed them.

A half-hour later they had completed a tour of one of the most enchanting, light-filled, innovative homes Max had ever seen—and had finally made the formal introductions he had intended to start with. "I've got to hand it to you, Jim," he said to the tall man who stood so possessively beside Meg and their daughter. "You've created quite a place here."

"Thanks," Jim answered. Then to Meg, "I'm going to check on dinner." He left them to walk into the kitchen.

"Jim's cooking tonight," Meg explained as he walked away. "And he's always modest about this place, but he did the whole design himself—even bought graph paper and drew the floor plans to scale before he turned it all over to a friend who's an architect. I framed his original plans and put them up on the wall of his office. You may have seen them on our tour."

"You're right. I did notice those. That's quite a talented guy you married," Max responded, choosing not to comment on Jim's cover-model looks or the tangle of blond mane that hung halfway down his back.

"You don't know the half of it," Meg responded with a glimmer.

For just an instant—only a second, really—Max felt a twinge of envy, thinking of the beautiful, unnamed woman by the roadside and wishing that someone, anyone, loved and admired him the way Meg obviously loved and admired her husband. Unaccustomed to such feelings, he shook it off, telling himself it had been a long day.

Jim came out of the kitchen to report that dinner would be ready in about half an hour, and Max decided that was adequate time to unload the car. Since Meg had already shown them which room would be his and which Marcie's, he carried their things directly into their new lodgings. They each took a few moments to unpack basics before Meg called them to dinner.

Max made his first faux pas as they sat down to eat. "Umm, this looks delicious, Jim," he said, and lifted the serving spoon to help himself to the rich, Italian-looking casserole.

Meg cleared her throat as Jim bowed his head and began to offer grace. Max quickly put the spoon down and waited to serve himself until after the "Amen." Then a few minutes later, as Max was enjoying a third helping of both casserole and salad, Meg announced that church was at nine and she'd expect everyone to be dressed and gathered in the living room by eight-thirty. That's when Max and Marcie both spoke at once.

"Mom says I don't have to go to church anymore."

"I'm not really much of a churchgoer, Meg."

Jim looked to Meg, who, with a patient smile, said, "This household goes to church at nine o'clock on Sunday mornings. We'll expect you to be ready at eight-thirty."

Max opened his mouth to protest, but Meg touched his hand as she murmured, "Think of it as a cultural experience, Max. It will be good for you and Marcie to attend church together," and he shut it again.

Marcie was not so easily quelled. "Daddy, do I have to?" she asked, her voice tuned to High Whine.

Max cleared his throat to buy time. "We'll try it tomorrow," he said, wondering it he wouldn't be better off to rent a small apartment for the summer—somewhere across town, maybe.

His third mistake came a while later when he sent Marcella in to bed.

"Aren't you going to go with her?" Meg asked.

His mind a blank, Max asked, "Why?"

"To chat a little, hear her evening prayers." He was still staring blankly. "At least tuck her in, Max."

"Oh. Oh, yeah," he said and followed Marcie down the hall, ruminating that he'd been right in the first place, and for more reasons than one. It was going to be a long, *l-o-n-g* summer.

Chapter Two

"**H**ey! Who said you could change the channel?"

"You know this is my favorite program. I watch it every Saturday."

"Give that back! Give that remote back!"

"Stop it, you little demon, before I give you the beating you deserve."

"Mom, Lydia's breaking the One-Mommy-Per-Person Rule again!"

"Quiet!" Cretia was shocked by the heat in her own voice. Apparently her children were, too. They both stared at her, eyes wide, mouths open. Having sworn she would never lose her temper in front of her kids, she made a point of counting slowly to ten before she spoke again, more quietly. "It's been a long day, and I think we're all tired. Danny, Lydia gets to watch this program because it's her favorite—"

"But—"

"And because you picked the last one. When this show is over, the TV goes off and everyone goes to bed."

"But it's Saturday!"

"And it's summer!"

27

"Mo-*ther!* It's only nine o'clock!"

"And the television is going off at nine-thirty," Cretia repeated, pleased to hear her voice both calm and firm. "Anyone who wishes to protest may get the time moved up half an hour."

Danny opened his mouth, then, at a wilting look from Lydia, quickly shut it again and flopped on the couch, arms folded tightly in front of him. Lydia sat at the far opposite side, too shocked by the early shut-off time to gloat over her small victory.

"Everybody remember we have church in the morning," Cretia added, taking advantage of the quiet moment. "I'd like us to be dressed and ready to go by at least twenty minutes till."

Lydia, already staring at the screen, mumbled, "Sure thing, Mom," in her most sarcastic tone, and Danny garbled out something unintelligible that Cretia took to be agreement.

Mesmerized by the silvery light from the corner, Cretia noticed that the television family Lydia so admired was getting ready to go somewhere together, too, only they had both a mother and a father gathering the troops and making preparations. For a moment—no more than a few seconds, really—she wished she had that kind of help available, someone warm and kind who would listen to her with the respect she got from Meg and would help her ride herd on her two-man gang of ruffians, someone like that kind, handsome man who had stopped to help her on the road this afternoon.

Cretia sighed, ending the thought. What was the point? She'd had her shot at the Cinderella story, and look what it had brought her. Aside from two great kids—the only part she did not regret—her marriage had brought nothing but heartache, followed by a fearful struggle to learn to live on her own, providing for herself and her children and trying to make a normal, decent life for them all. Now, thirty-one years old and burdened with responsibilities, she wasn't exactly the town belle anymore, and her chances of marrying again were no better than—

"Than finding a rainbow in the dark," she murmured.

"What?" Lydia asked, looking away from the TV.

"Nothing," Cretia answered, embarrassed to have spoken aloud. Then she decided to take advantage of this rare moment when she had her daughter's attention. "Oh, Lydia, remember that girl I told you about?"

"Meg's niece from L.A."

"Right. It's possible she could be at church tomorrow, if they're in town already."

"Okay. I'll keep an eye out for her."

"Thanks, hon." Cretia started for the hallway, ready for some peace. She'd put on some Mozart—"A Little Night Music," maybe—then soak in a hot shower and wrap up in a warm flannel nightie. Now *there* was one advantage to being single. She preferred not to think of the disadvantages.

"Oh, well," she mumbled, sighing.

"Did you say something, Mom?" Lydia called after her.

"Nothing, honey," Lucretia answered, smiling wryly to herself.

Max stretched and rolled his neck, then turned to look at the clock by the bedside. Sunlight streamed in through the eastern windows and he felt certain Meg must have changed her mind and let him sleep in. When he spotted the clock, he was surprised to see it was before seven. *I'm going to have to find out what kind of mattress this is*, he thought as he rolled out of bed. *I don't remember the last time I slept so well.*

Of course it hadn't been the "dreamless sleep" people always spoke of when they felt rested. His night had been filled with dreams, and his dreams had been filled with a dark-haired, dark-eyed woman with soft olive skin and a scent to die for. He found himself whistling happily as he showered and dressed for church, eager to begin his day.

" 'Rock of Ages, cleft for me. Let me hide myself in thee.' " Cretia sang along with the opening hymn, wishing she had managed to arrive a little early, as planned, instead of just as the meeting began. She scanned the congregation, looking toward the right front pews where she expected to find the McAllister contingent.

There they were, looking more like a convention than a family, everyone present except for big sister Joan, who lived in Winslow with her husband and kids. Wiley Richards sat with his new wife, Kate, former widow of James McAllister and mother to the clan. Wiley's daughter Sarah was at his other side between her father and her fiancé, Chris McAllister. Cretia realized with a small touch of envy that their wedding was only a few weeks away now. The parents had married first, and soon it would be their children's turn.

Next to Chris sat his brother, Kurt, Cretia's boss, with his wife, Alexa. Then beside them was oldest brother Jim with wife, Meg. Daughter Alexis sat with her daddy today.

Beside Meg was the teenaged girl who was the target of Cretia's speculation. In the little more than a week since she had arranged for Lydia to pal with Marcella, Cretia had generated all kinds of nervous fantasies about this "troubled child" from L.A.

She bit her lip as she studied the girl. Something about her sure looked familiar. Cretia could have sworn she'd seen her somewhere recently. *So that's Marcie*, Cretia thought with relief. *She looks pretty normal from here. From the way Meg talked, I was expecting green spiked hair and black leather.*

Not that she herself hadn't done plenty of odd things before she had settled into premature adulthood, Cretia amended with contrition. *Even green spiked hair isn't too terrible.* But it was easier to think that now that she had seen Marcie, and the child looked so pleasantly normal.

A man sat at the end of the row, next to the girl. *Must be Brother Max*, Cretia thought. Almost as if her thoughts had caught his attention, the man turned toward her, and she saw his face in sharp profile.

"Oh!" she gasped aloud, and people in the pews around her turned to see if she was all right. She smiled politely, her face warming with embarrassment. No mistaking where she'd seen *that* face before. It had haunted her dreams all night long.

She's here! Max thought, losing the words of the hymn. He hadn't stopped thinking of the woman for a moment, not even in his sleep. *Not that I'm looking, of course*, he reminded himself quickly. It wouldn't do to forget he wasn't good at relationships—especially not here, where he intended to spend so little time. *Wonder who she is?* he pondered. *I could ask Meg . . . no, better not. I don't want to spend the summer being pushed toward a woman. I'm being pushed enough already.*

He looked around him as he thought that, reminded of how Meg had practically strong-armed him into coming to church this morning. Still, he had to admit there was a pleasant familiarity about sitting in church again. It had been a long time since he had reminded himself of the solid, unchanging core of his often frantic life.

"Daddy, she's here," Marcie whispered beside him, and he followed her gaze, amazed to see she was looking at the same woman.

"I know, Marcie," he whispered back.

"She looks really nice today," Marcie added, and Max nodded eagerly.

It was only as he was shelving his hymnal that he risked a look over his shoulder and noticed the teenaged girl sitting beside the woman. Belatedly, he realized his daughter had been speaking of the girl, not her mother. Feeling both embarrassed and encouraged, he whispered to Marcie, "Maybe you can talk to her after church."

"Okay," Marcie answered, smiling, and in the privacy of his thoughts, Max smiled, too.

By the time the congregation had said its final *Amen* and the organist began the postlude, Max was already getting a stiff neck from turning to look back so often. He had repeatedly warned himself that the woman was going to get the wrong idea if he didn't stop staring at her. Yet he couldn't stop staring.

She really was attractive—young, probably not over thirty—with shoulder-length near-black hair, huge dark-chocolate eyes, and a touch of the Mediterranean in her warm, clear complexion. She was slim, though pleasantly rounded, and wearing a light summer dress in a shade of yellow-gold that made her seem to shimmer all over. No, Max couldn't stop himself from looking, and he couldn't help being pleased that, whenever he looked back, she was looking at him, too.

Now, as he started down the aisle, he was even more pleased to see her fighting the flow of traffic, walking toward him.

"Hi," she said as she stopped in front of him in the church aisle, and he warmed at the sound of her voice. "I want to thank you again for helping me with the car yesterday."

"No problem," he responded, more flattered than he'd been in ages and wishing he'd done something really spectacular with that car so she'd have more reason to be grateful.

Then she turned on one of those multi-megwatt smiles, and Max felt his mouth go dry. He had thought her attractive before. Now, with that flash of even, white teeth and her dark eyes brimming with warmth, she was positively breathtaking.

"You must be Max," she said, extending her hand.

"Uh, yeah." *Brilliant response, Carmody, but how does she know who I am?* He reached for her hand. It felt small and dry and very warm in his. "But how—?" he began.

"I'm Cretia Sherwood, and this is my daughter, Lydia," she said, drawing forward the girl he had seen. "My son, Danny, has already headed for the car. I think you met him yesterday."

"Um, hi," Max said again, nodding toward the girl and wondering if someone had forgotten to give him his copy of the script. "Cre-ja, is it?"

"Cretia," she answered, "short for Lucretia. Meg thought your dau—"

"I thought Marcie might enjoy having someone her own age to pal around with," Meg put in as she stepped up beside her brother. "Max, this is Cretia Sherwood. She works with me at the studio. And this is her daughter, Lydia. She's just a little older than Marcie." Meg reached toward her niece, drawing her attention from the baby, who was clowning in her father's arms. "Marcella, this is Lydia Sherwood."

The girls began chatting immediately, as if picking up in the middle of a conversation they must have started yesterday. The break gave Max a few precious seconds to recover from the disappointment he'd felt ever since the lovely lady (Cretia; her name was Cretia) had said his sister's name. He had hoped she was seeking him out just to make his acquaintance.

You should have known better, Carmody. What would a jewel like that see in an old fossil like you? he chided himself. Recovering his wits, he murmured, "Nice to meet you, Cretia," and dropped the woman's hand. His hand immediately felt alone and very empty.

"I thought maybe we could get the girls together after church today for a few minutes, if you don't have other plans . . ." Cretia began.

"Actually, we do have other plans," Meg spoke for him, and Max made a mental note to have a long chat with his overly pushy sister. "But you're welcome to join us, if you'd like. Lydia and Danny, too." *That helps,* Max amended. *Maybe I won't have to strangle Meg after all.*

"You know how the McAllisters get together on Sunday afternoons," Meg went on, her hand on Max's arm. "We're gathering out at the old farmhouse today. It's potluck. Just bring the kids and come."

Cretia looked uneasily at Max, as if hoping for his invitation. He kicked quickly into gear. "Yes, that would be great," he heard himself adding. "It will give the girls a chance to meet and talk, and maybe we can chat—you know, uh, compare schedules and things like that. I'd like to take another look at that carburetor, too."

"That would be great," Cretia said.

Meg looked from one to the other, one eyebrow raised. "I take it you two have met?"

"Not really," Cretia said, "but your brother rode in like the cavalry yesterday when my car broke down again."

"Again?" Meg huffed in frustration. "You really are going to have to junk that old thing."

"I know, I know. One thing at a time," Cretia said.

"Well anyway, we're on for the family dinner this afternoon, right?" Meg ventured. Cretia looked at the girls, already giggling in a center pew.

She nodded. "Okay then." Cretia looked from Max to

the girls and back again. "We're on for lunch. At the old farmhouse, you said?"

Meg nodded. "Um-hm. Where Chris is living now."

"What time?"

Max watched as the women ironed out the details. Throughout the sermon, while he'd been making a fool of himself staring over his shoulder at this lovely woman and imagining she was interested in him, it had never occurred to him that he might be able to spend the afternoon in her company. Okay, so the woman wasn't interested in him for his own sake. That didn't mean he couldn't enjoy just being around her, just standing close enough now and then to feel the warmth of her skin.

He made the necessary polite responses as the women confirmed plans and parted, but found his attention focused on the hypnotic glide of the figure in yellow-gold in front of him as he followed it down the aisle. Marcie was hanging on his arm and nagging him about something by the time they got to the car, but Max couldn't seem to focus on whatever it was. He was too busy remembering the charming, girlish dimple that had winked at him as Cretia said good-bye.

He'd looked. Okay, so it had been a long time since she'd been in the market for a man—at least, since she'd discovered she didn't *need* one to keep her family afloat—but she still knew what it meant when a man smiled that way, then looked from her face to her left hand and back again. What it meant to her was, Max Carmody wasn't just Marcella's dad.

She'd been attracted from the moment she'd first seen him riding to her rescue on the highway. What woman wouldn't be? His height and build contributed to a commanding presence and there was so much warmth in his smile. Then there were those sparkling blue-gray eyes and all that touchable brown hair, with just a smattering of distinguished gray at the temples. He was a woman's dream, all right, and it was a thrill to know he'd noticed her.

Of course there was no hope in it. Meg had told Cretia enough about her half brother that she knew he'd be headed back to Orange County as soon as the summer was over, if not before. *But a summer romance could be fun, too*, argued the little voice in the back of her head. *As long as you both keep your wits about you, anyway.* Cretia had to admit her little voice had a point. Even a light flirtation with an attractive man could go a long way to boost her once-flagging self-esteem and give a lift to an otherwise dull summer.

"Mom, Lydia says we're going to lunch at some farmhouse somewhere," Danny whined from the backseat, and Cretia turned her attention back to the moment.

"That's right, Danny. Out at Rainbow Rock Farms, where the McAllisters used to live. Chris McAllister still lives there."

"The pig place?"

She contained a beleaguered sigh. "Right, Danny. The pig place. You remember. We've had Sunday dinner out there before."

He rolled his eyes. "Yeah. I remember."

"Aw, come on, Danny. It'll be fun," Lydia chimed in.

"Fun for you, maybe."

He was pouting so hard, Cretia could feel it from the front seat. "I'm sure you'll find something to do," she added helpfully. "There are always some baby piglets or some new puppies or something to play with. If worse comes to worst, you always enjoy the big tire swing."

"Oh yeah, that's a real hoot." Danny had his sarcasm level turned up to high and Cretia had to bite her tongue to keep from giving him just the kind of response he was fishing for. Luckily for them both, Lydia was on her side this time.

"Maybe you could just sit on the porch and pout," Lydia offered. "That always seems to make you happy."

Cretia grinned in spite of herself, then fought the laughter out of her voice as she said, "Now Lydia, I'm sure Danny can handle this one on his own. After all, he's a big boy now." *And old enough to accept responsibility for entertaining himself this afternoon,* she added silently. After all, she wasn't going to have the time to entertain him. She had other plans. At least, she hoped she did.

Max had tried to keep his mind on his manners while visiting with Meg's extended in-laws and had made a point of figuring out which big blond hunk was which so he didn't confuse Meg's husband with his two brothers. Still, he had struggled with his concentration all through the opening civilities and was nervously pacing the front porch with the excuse that he "needed some air" by the time the worn-out old sedan turned onto the McAllisters' gravel road. *I'm not really that eager to see her again,* he lied to himself as he watched the car approach. *It's just that I have so little else to think about here. I'm going to have to get a hobby or something.*

He was pondering the possibilities for hobbies in Rainbow Rock when the car pulled into the dooryard and he stepped down from the porch to open the backdoor for Cretia's kids, who immediately scattered, the boy mumbling something about a tire swing.

"Are we the last to arrive?" Cretia asked as he opened her door, too. She had changed out of the yellow-gold sundress and now looked equally stunning in a pair of cinnamon-colored walking shorts that showed off her slim, long legs and a soft, off-white blouse.

" 'Fraid so," he answered. "Joan and Bob and their kids

got here a few minutes ago. We were starting to wonder if we'd have to send out the cavalry for you again.''

''Naw, just a tow truck.'' Cretia reached back into the car to lift out a big bowl covered in aluminum foil. ''I had trouble getting the old junker started.''

''Maybe I can have a look at it,'' Max offered.

''I'd appreciate that, Max, but not right now. At least let me feed you first,'' Cretia offered, and Max happily followed her toward the house.

''How do you come to know so much about cars, anyway?'' she asked as he led the way up the porch stairs. ''You aren't a mechanic, are you?''

Something in the way she said it suggested that if he were a mechanic, he'd be wise not to admit to it. ''I'm a mechanical engineer,'' he clarified, trying to make it sound more important than he thought it was. ''I design replacement parts for cars, then build them out of my factory in Tustin.''

Cretia's face lit up. ''I remember,'' she said. ''Meg told me about your factory.''

''Carmody Auto Parts,'' he said, aware that he was bragging. He was proud of the company he'd built.

''I think I've used some of your replacement parts before.'' She entered the house through the door he held for her. That brought them very close together, close enough he could smell the delicious scent of her. He felt woozy, but Cretia didn't seem to be sharing the sensation. He thought she was looking a bit nervous—skittish, maybe.

''We make brake parts and transmissions,'' Max said. ''The best ones available.'' When he tried to move nearer, she actually flinched.

''Yes, well, that's probably where I've heard your name before. Uh, will you excuse me?'' Cretia said, gesturing toward the bowl. ''I need to get this salad in the refrigerator.''

"Sure." Max nodded toward her and watched as she disappeared into the kitchen. *Was it something I said?* Max shook his head, wondering what he'd done to make her so eager to get away.

"Whew!" Cretia leaned against the refrigerator door, blowing out a sigh. Of course she'd known Max would be here before she came. She'd had the time since church to prepare herself to see him again. Still, nothing had prepared her for the sensory onslaught that had hit with hurricane force the moment she had seen him waiting for her, grinning, on the McAllisters' front porch. The first thing she'd felt was pleasure, and maybe a little smugness that this very attractive man was obviously waiting for *her*.

Then had come the heady sensations caused by the sheer power of him, the instant he had opened her door. He was a large man—over six feet tall, broad-shouldered, muscular, *big*. She had sensed the contained power of his physique, the force of his personality, the unquestioned magnetism of his masculinity. Then on top of all that, she'd learned he was a business powerhouse as well. Cretia's safety alarms were all shrieking now, warning her that this man was filled with power, so much that she instantly felt as if she could simply meld into him and be absorbed into all that mystical energy.

And that frankly scared her to death. She'd been vulnerable to the power of a man before. That he had actually turned out to be such a weak man was hardly to her credit, and she had learned the hard way that it could be a long and painful recovery when one took that kind of fall. She'd promised herself she would never make that mistake again.

So is that why I ran from Max just now? she asked herself. It was easy enough to find the answer. Max made her feel like a giddy schoolgirl—warm and flushed with heady sensations, tender and trusting and wanting someone to love and care for who would love and care for her in return. That made her as open to hurt and betrayal and violation of trust as she had been when she *was* a giddy schoolgirl and had felt all this once before.

So what do I do about it? she pondered, and this time there was no quick answer. One thing she did know: Figuring it out would be easier if she could keep her distance from Max.

She could hear the McAllisters milling about in the newly remodeled great room where Chris had taken out a couple of walls to combine the old living room, dining area, and parlor. They were setting up tables, putting chairs around and deciding who would sit where.

"Why don't you put Cretia here next to me?" she heard Max say, and she didn't know whether to smile or frown. "Then Marcie and Cretia's kids can sit right here at the end and we'll be close enough to keep an eye on them."

"That sounds fine," Kate answered, and Cretia sighed. Well, at least lunch should be interesting.

Max was relieved when Cretia came back from the kitchen, saw the space next to him that he indicated he had saved for her, and smiled in agreement. *Well, what did you think she was going to do, Carmody? Run screaming in front of all these people?* He had to admit it wouldn't have surprised him. He nodded to her as Kate enlisted various family members in setting the tables and putting out the food.

They were just about ready to be seated when the sounds of an engine in the dooryard alerted them to the arrival of another guest. A car door slammed, there were heavy, booted thuds on the front stairs, then a knock at the door. Chris called, "Alice, honey. Get that, would you?" and Joan's oldest daughter opened the front door.

The man at the door drew Max's attention immediately. Tall and well built, comfortably outfitted in boots and jeans, a western shirt, and a felt Stetson, his Native American ancestry written in his features, the man was a portrait of the modern American West. As the door swung open, he asked, "Am I late? Or is the invitation still open?"

"*Yah-ta-hey*, buddy!" Chris called. "Sure, it's open, especially if you brought food."

"*Carne asada*," the man answered in Spanish, and held up a roaster bag filled with ten pounds or more of barbecued meat. "Hot off the fire."

"Then welcome, indeed!" Chris called. "Hey everybody, Logan's here. You guys all remember Logan Redhorse, don't you? He's going to be the best man at our wedding next month."

Apparently everyone did remember Logan—except Max, of course—as Logan made the rounds, shaking hands and greeting them all. Max couldn't help but notice the way he greeted Cretia—rather too warmly, he might have thought—and the way she sparkled as she greeted Logan.

Okay, so there's a rival for the lady's affections, he said to himself, noting with irritation that Meg was seating the newcomer directly across from Cretia. *What? You thought no one else would have noticed a gem like that?* But his mood had soured considerably and he found himself wary of every move this Logan guy made. That alone should have ruffled his feathers. He had no right to claim Cretia, after all. *So why am I feeling so possessive so suddenly?* he asked himself, though he feared he might already know the answer. It had been years since he had responded so quickly and so completely to any woman. In fact, the last time he had felt like this was probably—

He almost succeeded in cutting off the thought. Almost.

Joanna. He had felt just this attracted, just this possessive about Joanna. And never since. *Well, that ought to tell you something, shouldn't it, Carmody? Just look what happened when you felt like this before. You gotta get some control here, buddy*. But when Logan held the chair for Cretia and helped her to be seated, when she looked up over her shoulder and turned that multi-megawatt smile on Logan instead of him, control was about the last thing Max felt. *Ah, well*, he thought, watching as they made small talk across the table. *At least lunch should be interesting.*

Interesting, Cretia thought as she watched the expression that crossed Max's face. *If I didn't know better, I'd swear the man is jealous. Jealous! Of Logan and me. Wow.* She almost mouthed that last word aloud. An interesting, attractive man like Max certainly had better things to do than stare at her while she made conversation with Chris's buddy, yet that was what he seemed to be doing, and his expression soured moment by moment as she smiled at something Logan had said or chuckled at a shared memory. She and Logan had never been anything more than friends, hardly even that before she began to work with members of the McAllister family, yet from watching Max, one would have thought . . . Well, it was probably better not to ponder what one would have thought. Still, Cretia couldn't help being flattered by the attention.

Would it be terribly mean of me to smile at Logan just a little more than usual, just to see what Max might do? she wondered, then tried it, and almost giggled as she saw Max's face darken. *Wow, indeed.* This lunch was turning out to be lots more fun than she'd planned.

Well, it has been interesting, Max reflected a half-hour later as he gazed at the engine of Cretia's old clunker. Even in this area he couldn't seem to win her undivided attention. The moment he had announced he intended to have a look at the car, he was swamped by helpful friends and family. Jim had come to help; so had Kurt and Chris and brother-in-law Bob. Max almost objected aloud when young Danny joined them, staring under the hood right along with the rest of them. "My dad's a mechanic," Danny said in explanation, and Max had answered, "oh," adding to himself, *At least that explains what Cretia has against mechanics.* Then of course, Logan had insisted on helping, too. *Does that guy have to be everywhere?* Max mumbled silently.

He reminded himself that he'd planned to learn what he could about Lucretia over lunch. *Let's see. What have I learned so far?* he thought sourly. He had learned that Logan was an attorney for the Navajo nation; that he had involved both Chris and Sarah in the commercial pig farm he had started on the reservation, and that was how the engaged couple had come to work together; that he had known Lucretia for several years, but had only come to work closely with her in the past two years or so; and that he had worked on her car more than once in the past.

He had learned very little about Cretia herself, except as it related to the handsome Navajo attorney, and they seemed to be "related" in one way or another quite a lot.

Face it, Carmody, he told himself as the assembled crowd of men pronounced the car beyond help and told Cretia as she joined them that she'd need a new one soon. *If this is a race, this Logan guy was already in the home stretch before you even got off the starting blocks.*

But was it a race? Why did he seem so determined to throw himself at a woman who obviously had other interests and other plans? To fight for a woman who lived where he'd hardly been willing to visit? To compete for one who already had children and a life and an agenda that didn't include him? One he would be leaving behind in no more than a few weeks' time?

Unwilling to ponder those questions too deeply, he busied himself with studying the makeup of the car's carburetor. When Lucretia asked despairingly, "Isn't there anything I can do to make this old bucket of bolts last a little longer?'' he concurred with the group's decision.

"Sorry," he told her. "With chewing gum and bailing wire, you might get through another few weeks, but I hear your winters get cold. You're going to want to replace this machine with something more reliable before the summer's gone.''

"Sorry, but he's right," Logan said, and Max gloated a little at having Logan back him. "You're going to need a new machine, Cretia." Max flinched at the sound of her name on Logan's lips. He seemed to speak it so tenderly.

Now you're imagining things, he chided himself as he closed the hood and followed the other men toward the house. *And anyway, if he's in love with her, how can you really blame him? If you weren't driving away in another couple of months, you might fall in love with her, too.*

Even as he thought it, his inner voice whispered that maybe he already had. "Oh, shut up," he muttered aloud. Let his inner voice mind its own business.

Chapter Three

Wwhat was he going to do about Cretia? How could he get her attention? And if he did, would he be able to walk away at the end of the summer? Max thought about his "Cretia problem" every time he woke up all night long, and because the questions also haunted his dreams, he awoke often. By the time he was ready to get up in the morning, he knew what he would do. It was simple, really, and brilliant if he did say so himself. Cretia needed a new car, so he'd get her one.

Feeling particularly pleased with himself, Max hummed a familiar Mozart melody as he showered and shaved, readying himself to take Marcella and Cretia's kids to breakfast, a promise he had allowed the threesome to coerce from him before he'd taken Marcie home yesterday.

They had also insisted on sleeping late—his concession to the beginning of their summer holiday—so he had read the classifieds section of the local weekly paper he'd appropriated from Jim, and marked all the ads for suitable prospects, before Marcie stumbled from her room. While she was getting dressed he called Nate Bailey at the auto parts plant, who cheerfully reported that production for the day was beginning well, so he was able to put that worry behind him, at least for the moment. By the time he had picked up Cretia's kids and packed the whole troop off to the Kachina Café, he was getting excited about beginning his car search.

He tried to be casual as he quizzed Cretia's kids over breakfast. "Has your mother done any car shopping?" he asked while handing Danny the ketchup for his home fries. "What kind of car do you think she'd like?" he questioned Lydia as he helped her blot up the water Danny spilled next to her plate. Though the kids weren't particularly help-ful, he felt he'd narrowed the options by the time they left the diner: no pickup trucks, no four-wheel drive, no auto-matic transmissions or power steering. Those last two con-fused him a bit, but he guessed she was opting for easy maintenance and high economy. He assumed she avoided the off-road vehicles so there would be no excuse for her to drive her own wheels into the out-of-the-way locations where Rainbow Productions frequently rolled tape.

He drove all three kids back to Cretia's house, promised to bring them a snack later, then started in with the first late-model sedan on his list. Around noon he called Nate again, who patiently reported that production for the day was moving nicely. He turned his attention back to the auto search and by three o'clock, he had found "the car," a nice-looking, clean, family sedan, only four years old with low miles and high economy. It even reminded him of Lu-cretia, lean and elegant. It was perfect for her, absolutely perfect.

Unfortunately the car's owner knew what a pearl he had and the price was a little higher than Max had counted on, even after negotiating his best deal. Still, it was so exactly right for Cretia. . . .

Frowning to himself, Max wrote out a check, then tried to be patient while the owner took him through the process of driving to the Rainbow Rock branch of the First National

Bank of Arizona, having the bank call Max's California bank at his expense, and making arrangements for the funds to be wired. "Sorry about that," the man, a Mr. McGee, said as they left the bank. "It's just, with you bein' from out of town and all, and me not knowin' you from Adam—"

"No apology necessary," Max assured him. "I'd have done the same thing." But he could remember a number of times when he'd taken checks from folks he'd never seen before. So far he'd done well, trusting people. That reminded him of his business in California, so he again called Nate, who dutifully reported that the production day was ending nicely, and that he himself would be able to get more work done if a certain owner would quit calling him every few hours from Arizona.

Max had had McGee fill out the necessary transfer papers in the name of Lucretia Sherwood (he had checked with Meg that morning to make sure he had the spelling right), so everything was in order by the time he pulled "the car" up in front of her home around four-thirty, just a little before he expected her to arrive. He'd brought a video to keep the kids busy—some silly teen horror flick, somewhat bloody, but with an acceptable rating—and he'd bought a bag of Popsicles to honor his snack promise, so the kids would be kept busy and out of trouble while he and Cretia checked out "the car." By the time she arrived at a little after five, he was keyed up and ready for the big surprise.

At least he thought he was. What he hadn't anticipated was the surprise in store for him.

"Hey, nice-looking car, Max," Cretia said as she got out of the clunker and started toward him.

"Thanks. I thought so," he answered, then dangled the keys in front of her. "It's yours."

She stopped stone-cold and gave him a blank look. "What?"

"I said, it's yours. Wanta drive it?"

"C-could you repeat that, please?"

He gave her an indulgent smile. "Cretia, meet your new car. Would you like to take it for a drive?"

She dropped her hands at her sides. "Max, what have you done?"

"You needed a car, so—"

"So you took it upon yourself to choose one for me? Like I'm incapable of picking my own?"

Somehow this was going all wrong. "That's not it at all. I just thought I could h—"

"You just thought you'd ride in like the cavalry again and save the poor damsel in distress, the poor stupid, helpless woman who obviously can't manage something like choosing a decent car—"

She was really getting wound up. Right through his disappointment and confusion, Max couldn't help but think how positively delicious she looked when her temper was fully aroused. "Hey, hey, give me a break here," he said, not sure whether he should put up his hands to defend himself or use them to try to soothe her—if he dared to touch her at all. "I'm the good guy in this scenario."

"Who says?" she asked, lifting her hands in a questioning gesture, then dropping them with a disgusted huff. "Men!" She turned on her heel and marched toward the house. She looked furiously angry—and positively wonderful.

"Now wait a minute," he said, dragging along behind her, working up more than a little indignation of his own. "It's not supposed to be like this."

"I don't know how it's *supposed* to be," Cretia said, turning on him, her eyes aflame, "but I'll tell you how it's going to be. Take your car and leave, Max. Go now." She turned toward the house, then back to him. "And you'd better take your daughter, too, while you're at it. That will keep you from having to come back later." She burst through the front door, slamming it behind her. A moment later Marcie appeared, carrying her things.

"Dad, Cretia says she'll return the video." Marcie seemed unflustered as she headed for "the car."

"Now wait a minute," Max said again. Who did she think she was, anyway, turning this all against him? He pounded on her door.

"Go away!" Cretia called from inside.

"Cretia, come on! I'm trying to do a good thing here," Max called, exasperated. "Can't we at least talk about this?"

There was a long silence before she came to the door. When she opened it, only a crack, her face showed hurt and disappointment. That got Max's attention. Had she still been so unreasonably angry, well . . . But she wasn't. And that was when Max finally understood. He hadn't meant to undermine her independence, or hurt her feelings, either. But clearly, he'd done both. He modified his tone. "Look, Cretia, I never meant to hurt your feelings, or to suggest that you couldn't do this yourself—"

"Then why did you think you had to do it for me?" He heard her voice quaver, as if she was about to break into tears.

"I knew you were busy, and I wasn't, so—"

"I can buy my own car, Max." She shut the door again, hard.

"Cretia . . ." he begged, knocking again. *Think, Carmody, think fast.* "I know you can buy your own car—"

"And what made you think I'd be willing to accept such an expensive gift from a man I hardly know?" she called from inside the house.

Gift. That's the key word. Come on, Max, think! "I hadn't intended it as a gift, really," he lied, vamping for time. "More like—like a trade maybe."

She cracked the door again and he could see the tears glistening in the corners of her eyes. "A trade for what?" Her tone accused him of a most ungentlemanly suggestion.

"For your old clunker," he said, hoping he could carry it off. It was all he could think of. "I figured we'd make a straight-across deal."

"You want my old clunker?" She seemed suspicious.

Of course she's suspicious, Max. Would you believe that one? "Yeah, I thought it might give me something to work on. You know, I can't spend all my time hanging around with the kids." *Hey, you're on a roll, Max*, he thought with some small pride. *This could work.*

She opened the door a crack more, her face hard with disbelief. "You want to work on my old clunker."

"Well, yeah. When you think about it, an old car is just a batch of used parts, all of them in one stage or another of wear, all needing replacement sooner or later. Carmody Auto Parts hasn't come up with a new replacement part in more than a decade." *Well, at least that part's true*, he thought, pleased with himself for quick thinking.

"Max, you know I can't accept a trade," Cretia said, but she opened the door more as she said it, and he could tell his arguments were wearing her down. "This car must have cost thousands of dollars—"

More thousands than I'm ever likely to admit to. . . .

"—and my junker isn't worth more than a few hundred, if I could sell it at all with the carburetor going out the way it is."

"That's true," he said, realizing he'd better concede something if he was going to keep this flowing in the right direction. "Maybe you'd consider a temporary trade? You drive the new car while I give the old one an overhaul and play with the various parts and pieces."

"And if the clunker is really unsalvageable, like you said yesterday?"

Darn it! Why hadn't he thought of that? Trust Cretia to remember. . . . "It may in fact be in just as bad a condition as we thought," he said, "in which case I'll try to persuade you to keep the new car for your trouble."

She paused, considering. "Only if you let me buy it."

Buy it! She couldn't afford what this car was worth. That was why he'd bought it for her in the first place. "Oh, I don't think that's really necess—"

"It's the only way I'll even consider it." She looked like she meant it.

"Why don't we just wait and see what happens?" he said, oh so reasonably.

"No. No way." She shook her head. "We come to terms now, or I send both you and that new car packing."

"Okay," he said, feeling trapped. "Then, if I can't restore the clunker, you can buy the new car—if you still want to by the end of summer."

"How much?" she asked, and he could see her bracing for the blow.

He hesitated before answering. He knew she couldn't afford what he had paid, what the car was really worth. Did she know enough about cars to guess if he underpriced it? Praying she didn't, he named a price that was about two-thirds of the check he'd just written.

"That much?" she said, wide-eyed, and he knew he'd guessed right.

"Of course I wouldn't expect you to pay that much," he added quickly, "what with it being a couple of months older by then and all. We can come to some fair arrangement, though, I'm sure."

She nodded. "Okay. We'll talk again in a few weeks. But if I don't like the deal, or don't want the car you've picked—"

"I won't hold you to any deal you aren't happy with." He smiled, trying to look reassuring.

"Well, okay then." She didn't look happy, but she did open the door.

He stifled a relieved sigh. "So okay then. *Now* would you like to take a drive?" Fishing in his pocket, he found the keys and held them up as before.

She paused, then smiled vaguely, nodding at him. "Yeah. Sure. Let's take a drive."

"Okay!" he said, feeling triumphant.

It took a minute to persuade the still unruffled Marcie that they weren't really leaving yet, then finally he and Cretia were in the front seat of "the car" together, taking it out for a spin as he'd planned from the beginning.

As they drove around the first corner, Max reminded himself of how little he knew of women and relationships. *I'm going to have to be more careful in the future*, he warned himself. For the moment, he chose not to see that he had just admitted to a future.

"Max, what were you thinking?" He had hardly seated himself at the dinner table before Meg started in. "Didn't you realize how it would offend Cretia if you went out and bought a car for her?" She set down the casserole she was carrying with a harder thump than seemed necessary.

"I . . . uh . . . how did you hear?"

Marcie walked in and began helping put out the flatware. She looked like the proverbial cat that swallowed the canary; Max could imagine yellow feathers poking out the corners of her mouth. "What?" she said, practicing her innocent look. "Was it supposed to be a secret?"

"I thought a car would be a nice surprise," Max answered, though it sounded lame now, even to him.

"I could have bought her a car last year," Meg said. "Jim and I talked about doing just that, but there are some things Cretia needs even more than a car, Max."

Jim entered the dining room then, and got out napkins

before he came to the table. Max realized he was the only family member, other than baby Alexis, who wasn't helping. He'd have to make a point of that at the next meal. "Has anybody talked to you about Cretia's background?" Jim asked.

"No, not really," Max answered.

"Let's sit down and say grace," said Jim, "then we can fill you in."

They were seated, Jim prayed, and Max remembered to say "Amen" before jumping into a discussion of Lucretia's life. Once it started, he found he was getting more than he'd bargained for. "So she had it pretty tough," he observed after he'd heard more stories about alcoholism, abuse, and an ugly divorce than he wanted to hear.

"It wasn't just the difficult moments," Meg said. He noticed she'd adopted the same tone one used when explaining a difficult concept to a small child. "It was the little things that happened every day that made her feel helpless or incompetent, like she couldn't possibly live without someone to take care of her."

"I'm afraid that's a tool many insecure men fall back on," Jim said. "They're afraid their women will leave if they think they can manage alone. Their only way to guarantee cooperation is to undermine the confidence of their women so they don't feel capable of managing alone."

Max nodded, remembering how he'd felt when he'd seen Cretia's hurt look. "And I did the same thing when I let Cretia believe I didn't think she could pick a car for herself," he murmured, half to himself.

"I'm afraid so," Meg said. "Kurt and I have been watching this car situation since Cretia first came to Rainbow Productions. She's learned so fast, and has become invaluable to us, and we've raised her salary as fast as we dared without further undermining her by making it seem like a gift. I've been hoping that with this next promotion to field producer, she'd be able to afford to buy a car on her own. I think she's been counting on it.''

"So I took that away from her, too." Max was crestfallen.

Meg took his hand. "Look, Max, I know you meant well, but—"

He cut her off. "Wait. Did our little informer here—" He paused, turning a disgusted look on his daughter. "Did she tell you how we settled things?"

Meg looked from Max to Marcie. "Maybe you'd better tell us," she said.

So Max explained how he'd talked Cretia into accepting a trade, and how she'd agreed to buy "the car" if he couldn't get the clunker into acceptable repair by summer's end.

"Well, it sounds like you managed to leave her a little dignity," Meg said as he finished, and he flinched slightly, thinking how badly this had gone. *You're going to have to learn to think these things through, Carmody*, he told himself sternly. *Otherwise, you could spend yourself into bankruptcy and end up the heel because of it.* That thought struck him as funny and he chuckled, drawing Meg's attention.

"Did I miss something funny?" she asked.

"Yes," he said, choosing to remain mysterious. "Yes, I think you did," but as he turned away, he made another mental note to keep more of his thoughts to himself, especially around his highly perceptive sister.

"Where do the clean forks go?" Max asked. Following his own advice, he was helping with dinner cleanup, pitching in with the rest of the family. He'd already called Nate, who had testily reported that the production day had gone just fine and that if he called four times again tomorrow, he might just have to find a new production manager.

"Here," Meg said, pulling out a drawer full of flatware

in neat compartments. "Thanks for the help, Max. I think we're going to start letting you and Marcie cook one night a week. How does Thursday sound?"

"Uh, okay, I guess." Max tried not to sound too shocked. Except for boiling water and warming takeout in the microwave, he couldn't remember the last time he'd even been in a kitchen. He wondered how quickly he could excuse himself from this one. Some soothing Mozart melodies sounded good about now.

"Okay, Thursday it is then." Meg handed him another stack of flatware as she spoke. "Let me know if you need anything special at the store."

"If I need anything special, I'll get it myself," he growled, asking himself how he kept getting conned into these things.

But apparently Meg was only getting started. "Jim and I thought you and Marcie might join us in a game of Rook this evening," she said as Jim reached past him to put some knives in the cutlery block.

"I think you'd get a kick out of it," Jim put in.

Given the other things Meg had volunteered him for, Max doubted it. "What's Rook?" he asked suspiciously. To himself, he added, *Well, so much for Mozart*. He almost sighed aloud.

"It's a card game, Dad," Marcie chimed in as she loaded glasses into the dishwasher. "Lydia was teaching it to me when you came this afternoon."

"A card game, huh?" Max hadn't had any special plans for the evening, other than a little quiet music and some thinking time in his room, but at the moment, anything sounded better than playing cards with the family. "Well, I don't know—"

"It's more fun when you play partners," Meg said. "You and Marcie can team up, Max. You can play against Jim and me."

"Oh, yeah, that sounds fair." Max liked the idea less the more he heard. "Let's partner the two old pros against the newbies and see who wins."

"You'll be surprised how fast you can catch on," Jim said, apparently unfazed by Max's sarcasm. "We'll play a couple of practice hands so you can get the hang of it, before we start keeping score."

So that was how Max found himself seated at the dining room table across from his daughter, looking at a hand of Rook cards, their numbers gleaming at him in suits of black, green, red, and yellow.

"It's a little like contract bridge," Marcie said as they began the first practice hand. "You bid on how many points you think you can take—"

"Or that you think you and your partner can take, when you're playing partners," Meg added.

"—and then, if you have the high bid, you get the card in the widow and you get to declare trumps," Marcie went on.

"You also take the first lead," Jim added. "And don't forget to discard. We won't warn you when it's not a practice hand. If you forget to discard, you go set."

"Go set?"

"Lose your bid. That means we subtract whatever your bid was from the points you've accumulated," Jim answered.

"Or from zero, if that's where you stand," Meg said, egging him on. "You also go set if you can't make your bid. Okay, the first team to reach five hundred wins."

"Okay," Max said.

"We'll play local rules," Meg said, dealing the last of the cards for their practice hand. "The one is high. The Rook is the low trump. Everybody ready?"

"Yeah, right," Max said, unable to remember most of

what he'd just heard. He settled in to try to figure out the game.

This really isn't as tough as it seemed at first, he thought later as he raked in a hand he had just taken with a black nine, black being the trump Marcella had declared. In fact, he was surprised to realize he was actually having fun.

Marcie is a pretty darn good partner, too, he realized as Meg and Jim topped five hundred and "went out" the winners, with his team less than fifty points behind. *She's a bit too conservative in bidding—she had some hands I certainly would have bid on—but sharp in piling on the points in a hand she knew I'd take and cautious in leading a high card our opponents might trump. I enjoyed playing with her.* That was even more of a revelation.

"I had fun tonight," Marcie said a few minutes later as he walked her to her room. "You're a pretty good partner, Dad."

"So are you, kid," Max answered, patting her back.

"Good night, Daddy," Marcie said, then in a move so quick he almost missed it, she went up on her toes and gave him a soft kiss on the cheek. "I love you."

"Good night, Marcie," Max answered, surprised by the huskiness in his voice. "I, uh, I love you, too."

Marcie smiled up at him as she closed her bedroom door. Max felt that smile pull tightly all around his heart.

He was up early the next morning, unable to sleep past dawn, and out the door shortly afterward. If he was going to work on Cretia's old clunker, he was going to have to find a place. He thought about calling Nate, decided against it, then put on a favorite disk of Mozart concertos and hummed along with the familiar tunes as he cruised up and down the streets of downtown Rainbow Rock, such as it was, looking for a mechanic's shop or commercial garage. . . . "Or someplace just like that," he said aloud,

stopping his red convertible in front of a likely looking spot
with a couple of mechanic's bays and a back wall covered
in tools and equipment.

It was open for business and already had a pickup and
a small sedan up on its hoists before he arrived at a little
after eight-thirty. That alone made it look like a thriving
business. Still, he'd never met a mechanic who complained
of having too much business, or too much money. This
looked like a good place to make a deal.

"Hi," he said, singling out the man under the pickup.

Middle-aged, a bit paunchy around the middle and bald-
ing on top, the man looked out from under the pickup's
engine. "No customers allowed in the shop," he said
shortly.

"I'm not a customer," Max answered, "at least not yet.
Are you the owner?"

"Yeah." The man turned, offering Max a challenging
look. "Who wants to know?"

"The name's Max." He extended his hand.

The man stepped out from under the truck, wiped grease
from his hand on a small towel attached to his belt, and
offered his own hand. "D. J.," he responded. "What can
I do for ya, Max?"

So Max sketched his situation, eliminating names and
relationships. He got only partway through when the man
interrupted him. "I don't loan out my tools—" he began.

"I wouldn't either, if they were mine," Max assured
him. "But it's not just your tools I want."

He went on, briefly explaining what he was looking for.

"So you're just in town for a few weeks," D. J. said,
"and you're looking for a place with tools where you can
pick apart an engine."

"That's about the size of it," Max answered, then
reached into his wallet and pulled out a roll of hundred-
dollar bills. "I'm willing to pay rent."

The sight of that many hundreds in one place apparently erased any concerns D. J. had about his space or equipment. They concluded the deal quickly after that, with D. J. explaining what hours he was open and that he didn't have space for Max to bring in the whole car. "But you can set up the engine on that back counter there, and come in to work any time I'm here."

"That's great," Max said. "It's a deal then." He counted out the money for the few weeks' rent and a little extra they'd agreed on for a security deposit, in case any of D. J.'s tools should end up lost or damaged. "Oh, and one other thing," he added, remembering how Danny had asked permission to work with Max on his mother's engine. "There's a boy who'd like to work with me. Okay if I bring him along?"

"A boy? How old?" D. J. asked.

Max paused, scratching his head. "I'm not sure. Maybe ten or eleven."

D. J. shook his head in response. "Sorry, man. No can do. My liability insurance is through the roof as it is. Part of the deal I agreed to was I wouldn't have customers in my shop, or anyone under the age of sixteen workin' here. I wouldn't consider havin' any kid but my own in here, and I'd only allow him because I know I'm not gonna sue me if somethin' happens."

Max had to chuckle at that. "I know what you mean. I own a business back home in California, and liability insurance is one of my highest costs."

"Getting to be so a decent man can hardly afford to be in business anymore," D. J. said, and the two men struck up a congenial conversation that ended with a handshake on their deal.

As Max walked away, he was thinking how perfectly everything was working, what a great place to work he had found, and how he liked doing business on a handshake.

This D. J. guy wasn't like him, not in many ways, but there was a camaraderie among working men that made them brothers. Max found he liked that.

Marcie had showered and eaten breakfast by the time he got back to Meg's place, so Max drove her into town to spend the day with Cretia's kids. He apologized to Danny that it wasn't going to work out for him to get in on the tinkering, then headed out to Rainbow Rock Farms to talk with Chris McAllister. By noon he had driven Cretia's old clunker up next to Chris's farrowing barn, where the body of the old veteran would remain while he tinkered with its heart. Using the block and tackle Chris used for moving heavy loads of hay, he pulled the engine from the car and settled it into the back of Chris's pickup for the ride to town.

"Wish I could help you at the other end, buddy," Chris said as he handed Max the keys, "but I've got a sow in here getting ready to drop her litter. She had trouble last time and I think I'd better hang around in case she needs help. Think you can handle it alone?"

"No problem," Max answered, though he couldn't yet imagine how he'd manhandle the heavy engine by himself. "I'll get your truck back before too long."

"Take your time." Chris waved off any suggestion he might be in a hurry. "As long as I'm tied up with Flossie here, I'm not going anywhere."

"And if you need help?"

"I call my fiancée." Chris grinned. "There are advantages to marrying a veterinarian into the family."

"Yes, I can see that. Well, good luck to you and, uh, Flossie."

"Thanks." Chris popped inside the barn.

Max fired up the pickup truck and headed for town, wondering what he'd do next. It wasn't like home, in Tustin, where he could just order several of his employees to leave their other work for a minute until the engine was moved. *I'm going to have to find a phone and give Nate a call*, he thought miserably. Here, out of his element, he knew no one he could call. No one at all. Not even—

"What's Logan Redhorse doing here?" he mumbled aloud as he pulled up in front of the garage where he'd paid D. J. for space. He waved a reluctant acknowledgment as the tall Navajo man raised his hand in greeting.

"*Yah-ta-hey.*" Logan greeted him in Navajo as Max walked toward the garage.

" 'Morning," Max answered. "What brings you here?"

"I just had Danny here install a winch in the back of my truck," Logan answered, jerking a thumb at the garage. "Seems I keep getting called upon to pull people out of snowdrifts and mires and such."

Max recalled hearing the tale of how Logan had rescued Chris and Sarah during a freak snowstorm last month. Just afterward they had announced their engagement. "I think I heard something about that," Max muttered, looking enviously at Logan's new winch. Of all the people in the world he might want to ask for help, the man he saw as his primary rival was probably in the bottom ten or so. Still . . .

"Look. You gonna need some help moving that engine into the shop?"

"Well, yeah." He certainly hadn't expected Logan to volunteer. "Do you mind?"

"No problem. I can give the new winch a test run. Let me just check with Danny to see if that's okay." He stepped back into the shop.

Danny? Max wondered. *Must mean D. J. Or maybe the guy who works for him?* He didn't get a chance to ask because Logan was back within seconds. With Logan's winch positioned between Chris's truck and the workbench where the engine was going to rest, it took very little time for the two men to wrestle the heavy engine into place.

"Thanks," Max offered, trying not to show the reluctance he felt. Of all the men to be indebted to . . .

"No problem." Logan looked at Chris's truck. "Guess you need to take that back to the farm, huh?"

"Yeah. I think I'll take care of that right now."

"Got a ride back into town?" Logan asked.

"Yeah. Yeah, my car's out there." Max almost shuddered at the thought of owing Logan another favor.

"Okay then. See you around."

"Yeah. Thanks again." Max waved an awkward farewell. *Why do I feel like such a heel?* he wondered as he started up Chris's truck. *I really am grateful for Logan's help. Don't know how I'd have moved that engine without him. Just . . . why did it have to be Logan?* He had watched the way the big man moved as they muscled the engine around. Logan was all the things Max had once been— young, lean, strong, graceful. *Can I blame Lucretia if she's attracted to that?* he asked himself, already knowing the answer. *And when I drive back to Tustin next August, Logan will still be right here.* A cold shudder went down his spine as he thought it.

"So when you comin' back to work on that engine?" D. J. asked from behind him.

"I'll be back within an hour, two at the most," Max answered, still watching as Logan's truck took the turn onto Navajo Boulevard.

"See ya then," D. J. said.

Max nodded an answer, then got in Chris's pickup still thinking about Logan, wishing he could manage to like him less. *I'm going to have to call Nate to check on production,* he told himself as he drove away.

Chapter Four

Cretia steered the slim, golden sedan into the driveway of her home and eased it to a stop. She'd been driving the car—Max's car—for four days now, ever since he'd presented it to her Monday evening. She'd had little choice since she'd agreed to surrender the clunker.

Max's car. She reminded herself to remember that. *Best not to even start thinking of it as mine.* She hadn't begun to forgive Max for the high-handed stunt he'd pulled in choosing it for her without even asking her advice or consent. *Who does he think he is, anyway?* she asked herself, taking her temper out on the emergency brake as she jerked it into place.

Max's car. Too bad it's such a beauty. Okay, so Max had chosen the car when he had no right. She didn't plan to forget that. But she couldn't help but notice how perfectly he had suited the choice to her needs and tastes. *It's just what I'd have picked if I'd found it myself*, she admitted, if only to herself. *That is, assuming I could afford anything this nice.*

It was everything she had wanted: recent model, low mileage, high economy, easy maintenance. It was even suited to her specific tastes: manual transmission, standard brakes, plenty of room for the kids, and a stylish look that made her feel good about being seen in it. She even liked the elegant gold color. The clincher, of course, was the tape of Mozart concertos that Max, or someone, had left in the cassette player. It had started on one of her favorite pieces the first time she turned the key in the ignition. Perversely, that had made her even angrier. *Who is he to choose something so perfect for me?* she argued. *I hardly know the man.* Pointedly, she ignored the little voice that hinted she might like to know him better.

Feeling more perturbed by the minute, and more out of sorts with Max, Cretia stepped through the kitchen door and set her bag of groceries on the kitchen counter, then went in search of her kids, only to find them saving the world from alien attackers on the TV screen, with Marcie and the aforementioned troublemaker cheering them on.

Cretia paused, watching them from the doorway while her heartbeat returned to a more normal pace. *They certainly look comfortable together*, she couldn't help thinking. *As if they were meant to be together like this.* She recognized that thought as dangerous and shook it away, then cleared her throat to announce herself and settled on the couch near where Max lay stretched on the floor with his back against the sofa, his long legs practically filling up her small living room.

"I'd have thought you two would be long gone by now," she said quietly, careful not to disturb the concentration of her two space rangers, who by now were the only defense protecting Earth from immediate conquest.

"We would have been, except for this late-in-the-day assault from outer space," Max agreed amiably, careful to keep his voice down. "Then, too, there's a movie showing in Holbrook that I thought the kids might like, but when I suggested it, they thought we should invite you, too." He interrupted himself at that moment to cheer and applaud a particularly good move Lydia had made, taking out the alien mother ship in a spectacular explosion and winning the game. Then he turned his attention back to Cretia. "So you're invited. Wanta go see a movie?"

"Um, I see." A movie? With Max and the kids? It wasn't what she'd planned for the evening—well, all she'd really planned was some quiet music and an early bedtime—but now that she thought of it, it did sound like fun. . . .

"So what d'ya think? You wanta come see a movie with us?" Max prodded.

Cretia had noticed the marquee on the Holbrook theater as she was driving out of town. The theater was playing a light, romantic comedy of the sort she had always enjoyed. Just minutes ago, she'd been noticing that title and thinking how fun it would be to go out to a movie for a change, but it hadn't occurred to her to take her kids, and it certainly hadn't occurred to her to invite Max. How would she feel about sitting so near him during the tender, romantic scenes? Just sitting here, in her living room with the universe exploding around them, she was already acutely aware of him.

Max tapped his watch in a playful gesture. "I was thinking we might go tonight?"

She smiled. *Well, why not?* "That sounds like fun. What time does it start?"

"Seven," Max answered.

"And it's a quarter to six now. Gosh, I'll have to hurry if I want to get us some dinner." She leaned forward as if to stand.

Max caught her hand. "No need for that. We can pick up fast food on the way. I'll treat."

"No. I can't allow that, Max." She shook him away, too aware of how good his palm felt pressed against hers. *After all, I'm going to have to take a stand somewhere. How much can I accept before I begin to feel obligated?* She stood, steeling her voice. "I planned a big dinner salad, and dinner salad it shall be. I can have it on the table in fifteen minutes or less."

Max seemed uncertain. "You're sure that's what you want to do? Really, it would be easy to grab burgers or chicken or something—"

"This will be just as fast and much more nourishing," Cretia insisted. "Time me if you don't believe me about the speed." She started for the kitchen.

Max put up his hands in a gesture of surrender. "Okay, okay, I believe you, but it will be even faster if I help." He stood, preparing to follow.

"You? Help?"

"You wound me, madam," he said, grabbing at his chest in a melodramatic gesture. "If you'll just point me at whatever it is you want me to do—"

"Honestly now, are you any good in a kitchen?" She had her doubts.

"Not much," he admitted, "but Marcie and I cooked for the household last night."

"Whoa, that must have been something to see." Cretia started emptying the grocery bag.

"It wasn't bad, thanks to Marcie," Max said. "We baked some chicken breasts with cream of chicken soup and instant rice. It's a recipe she learned in her seventh-grade Foods course. Of course, dinner was kind of late—"

"I'll bet it was good, though," Cretia said, choosing to give him a break. She handed him a head of lettuce. "Here. You can wash that if you like, then core it and rip it into bite-size chunks."

"Core it?" He couldn't have looked more lost or uncomfortable.

"Here." Cretia took pity on him. She washed the lettuce herself, then showed him how to pull the core by popping the head against the edge of the sink and drawing the core out. "Then break it up into little chunks," she said, demonstrating that as well. "You can put them into that big bowl on the counter."

"Okay," Max said as he began the process.

Cretia watched from the corner of her eye as she sliced cucumbers, tomatoes, peppers, and cheese, as well as some leftover chicken from last night's dinner. Max's moves betrayed some of the awkwardness of inexperience, as she might have expected, but even in that he was graceful, moving with an ease and economy of motion that Cretia found admirable, even attractive. And it felt easy and comfortable to work beside him in her kitchen.

Careful, Cretia! she warned herself. Given the direction her thoughts were taking, even three curious teenagers might be inadequate as chaperons. She turned her attention to the task of getting a salad ready in record time.

Less than twelve minutes later, they sat down to eat. Cretia asked Max to say grace and he spoke a warm and apparently heartfelt prayer, with gratitude for "the company of good friends" and "time to enjoy our lives." Then as they ate, he complimented her on the salad. "You were right. It was as quick as any fast food we might have picked up, and it's delicious, clearly better for us than greasy burgers or chicken."

"Thank you," she answered, pleased.

"But Cretia," he added, his eyes twinkling mischief, "can I buy these kids some greasy burgers or chicken later this summer? Just so they can have the all-American experience, you understand."

She grinned. "I understand. We'll count on that, sometime later this summer." It pleased her to know he was thinking ahead, planning her and her children into his future—for a few weeks, anyway.

As they loaded their children into the car—*Max's car*, she reminded herself firmly. *His child; my children*—it occurred to her that they looked much like the family from Lydia's favorite Saturday evening sitcom, loading up for a family outing. *Watch it, Lucretia!* she warned herself. *You're getting carried away here.* Still she couldn't help but notice how easily and comfortably everyone fit together. It would have been difficult for an outsider to tell they weren't a family. *Stop it! Do you hear me? Stop it!* she ordered.

"Hey, everybody. Look!" Danny called from the backseat. "We look just like a family!"

Max caught Cretia's eye and she quickly turned away, afraid her emotions were showing all over.

They were an hour into the movie when the leading man leaned toward his lady, his expression intense and laced with passion. Cretia flashed Max a quick glance from the corner of her eye. Seeing his eyes riveted to the screen, she looked back at the movie, anticipating that on-screen kiss.

Heavens! I haven't felt like this since—

She cut herself off. *Since Danny. Since high school. Since I was far too young to know better.* She couldn't quite stifle the sigh that broke from her as the screen couple came together, first in a tentative touching of lips, then in a deeper kiss, then in an embrace that just about knocked her breath away. It didn't help at all when Max caught her hand, gripping it in his, letting his touch tell her he was thinking all the same thoughts.

I'm going to have to keep my wits about me, she warned herself firmly. *I'm going to have to think of some way to keep this under contr—*

"Mom, I've gotta go to the bathroom."

Cretia almost laughed aloud. *Trust little Danny to throw ice water on a delicate moment.* "Go ahead and go," she whispered.

"I'm scared to go by myself," Danny whined. She heard Max chuckle and knew he was as caught up in this irony as she was.

"Okay, I'll walk out with you. Ask your sister to move over."

Max touched her shoulder. "I'll take him," he said.

"No, I'll go with him. You don't need to miss the movie," she answered, already standing. *Besides*, she added only to herself, *I need a break from all that romance.*

Danny took his time in the rest room. When they finally returned to the movie, the leading man and his lady were back to the action-adventure sequences, hacking their way through thick rain forest and trying to outsmart the bad guys.

It's just as well, Cretia thought as she settled in next to Max. But there were no bathroom interruptions several minutes later when the characters had foiled the villains and were rewarded with time alone together to enjoy the spoils of their victory, and each other. Cretia found herself struggling to shake the mood that hung over her as the house lights came up. She dared not quite look Max in the eye as she made her way into the center aisle and out toward the lobby.

"Good movie, huh, kids?" Max asked as they loaded into the car.

"Yeah," Danny answered. "I especially liked the part where they got the machine gun away from the bad guys and started shooting all the tires out from under the getaway cars." He braced his arms in gunner position, mimicking the sound of the firing as he mowed down everything in the parking lot.

"I liked the love scenes," Marcie said, her voice dreamy. She slid into the backseat next to Lydia.

Me, too, Cretia thought. Aloud she said, "Get into the car, Danny. You've done in enough imaginary bad guys for one evening."

"Okay, just one more," Danny said, mowing down the owners of the sport utility vehicle to their right and drawing looks of disapproval from both the man and woman.

"They're probably childless," Max murmured to her as the couple drove away, the woman still glaring over her shoulder.

"And therefore know everything about how to raise children," Cretia answered, sharing the joke.

Max chuckled and turned to the backseat. "It's still early," he said. "What say I treat everybody to root beer floats?"

The question brought cheers from the backseat and a furrowed brow from Lucretia. "Not fair," she said. "You get them all on your side before you even ask me."

He wiggled his brows in a knowing gesture. "Safety in numbers."

"Unfair," she answered, more adamantly.

"So how about it? Could you go for a root beer float?" She thought Max looked just a bit too confident with the kids chanting, "Root beer, root beer, root beer" from the backseat.

"Okay," she answered, "but let's buy some root beer and ice cream and take them back to our house. We'll make our own floats there."

"Great!" Danny said, anticipating. "That way we can have as much as we want!"

"That way," Cretia corrected, "I can make sure you don't pig out and stay up half the night with a tummy ache."

"Aw, Mom," Danny answered. "You know I don't get tummy aches anymore."

"Not since last month, anyway."

"That was just 'cause I rode the Graviton at the fair," Danny whined.

The conversation kept them busy all the way to the grocery store, where Cretia left Max to ride herd on the kids while she bought the goodies for their evening treats. Max said he wanted to go in instead, but Cretia insisted, determined to pay for part of the evening's entertainment, and telling Max aloud that since this was his idea, he could just deal with the consequences. She wasn't gone long, but she could tell something about the mood in the car had changed by the time she returned.

"Mom, we've been talking while you were gone," Lydia announced as Cretia opened the door.

"Uh-oh," Cretia answered. "Why don't I like the sound of that?"

"No, it's a good idea, really," her daughter insisted. "Marcie and Mr. Carmody have been learning to play Rook. I just thought we could play a game tonight at our house."

"We'll play family teams," Marcie said. "You and Lydia against Dad and me."

"Sounds great to me," Max chimed in.

"What do I get to do?" Danny whined.

"You can keep score," Cretia answered, belatedly realizing she had just given her consent. "Sure," she answered. "Sounds like fun. Maybe we'll play a short game, though. Say, one or two hands?"

In the end, they played a full game, clear to five hundred, with Max and Marcie edging out Cretia and Lydia by only twenty points in the final hand. "You two learn quickly," she conceded as the kids scattered and Max stood to help her tidy the table and put the game away.

"It's fun," Max answered. "And I'm finding that Marcie has a good head for strategy."

"She does," Cretia agreed, realizing for the first time how little Max must have known about his daughter before this last week together. "Are you enjoying your time with her?"

"You know, I am," Max admitted. Cretia thought he seemed almost grudging. "At first I thought I'd go crazy in this little town. I called my plant manager so many times, he threatened to quit if I called him again. Then I decided to tear your old car down just to have something to do—and I am working on it," he reassured her quickly. "Don't think I'm not. It's just that, the last couple of days, I've hardly even thought about bugging my production manager about how the plant is doing. Instead I find I'm hanging around with the kids more and running off to work on the clunker—uh, your car, I mean—a little less every day." He gave her a beseeching look. What he *looked* was absolutely marvelous. "You don't mind too much, do you?"

"Mind you spending time with the kids? Of course not! I'm delighted they have some adult supervision during the day."

He turned that beseeching look into a sheepish grin. "Even when that adult is playing video games and buying them root beer floats?"

"Well," Cretia agreed with a smile, "you have to admit you were setting me up to be the bad guy if I didn't agree with you on that one."

"Guess I was at that," Max said. "Sorry," but he didn't look too sorry. He looked rather pleased with himself—smug, even.

Cretia started toward the kitchen with a used napkin she meant to throw into the trash container. Then she thought better of it. "Look," she said, turning back to Max, but he had been following her and her sudden turn brought her right into his arms. "Oh!" she said as he caught her elbows, steadying her, then somehow his arms were around her and she was staring up into his face, his expression just like the one she had just seen on the face of the movie hero just before he—

"Cretia." Her name sounded so gentle on Max's lips, his luscious-looking lips. He leaned toward her.

"Max, I—"

"Mom, Lydia's breaking the One-Mommy-Per-Person Rule again!" Danny burst into the kitchen, charged with some grievance that needed immediate intervention.

Cretia swallowed hard, staring into Max's eyes, mirth crinkling the corners of her mouth.

Max blinked twice, his own eyes twinkling, then slowly released her.

She turned toward her son. "I'm sorry, Danny. What did you say?"

Danny looked from one adult to the other. "Wow," he said reverently. "Were you two, like, kissing or something?"

Max made a gruff sound in his throat and Cretia flashed him a warning look. "What can I help you with, Danny?" she asked, oh so patiently.

She barely heard his complaint about something or other that Lydia had done, barely heard herself giving some kind of rote response about him having more patience and trying to work things out with his sister, barely remembered to tell him to get dressed for bed as he headed back down the hall. Though her face was turned toward Danny, her attention was riveted on the man at her side, her body as tense as a drawn bow while she waited for Danny to leave the room. When they were finally alone again, she turned to Max, heart pounding. "You know," she said softly, "we can't count on Danny to interrupt us every time we're about to do something we'll regret."

"Oh, I don't know," Max said with what seemed like exaggerated calm. "He's doing pretty well so far. And besides"—he turned, stroking her arm and sending little shivers up and down her—"are you so sure we'll both regret it?"

She dropped her lashes. "I'm afraid I will."

He lifted her chin, looked into her eyes. "I won't do anything you don't want, Lucretia. I won't push you for anything you don't want to give, or make you regret any time you spend with me."

"But you will leave at the end of the summer."

He paused, blinked again, as though walking into bright light. "Well, yes. We both understand this situation is just temporary."

"I'm not sure I can do that, Max." She looked up into his eyes, lifted her fingers to touch his cheek. "I'm not sure I can do . . . temporary. If I let myself like you, if I let myself care, I'm not going to want to let you go."

He paused. To Cretia, he looked like a man carefully weighing every thought, every word. "Then we have something of a situation here, don't we?"

She couldn't help smiling. "Looks like we do."

"The question is, What do we do about it?"

"Hmm," she said. "Good question."

"All it needs now is a good answer," Max said. The whole time they'd been speaking, he'd been drawing her nearer, and nearer. Now he spoke with his lips only inches from hers. "Let's try this for a start," he said, closing that distance.

Cretia felt the breath go out of her in a whoosh as Max's lips touched hers. The attraction that had been budding within her blossomed as she gave herself to that kiss. She was unaware of putting her arms around Max, or drawing him closer, yet somehow her arms were around him and she was holding him as tightly as she knew how to hold.

She couldn't remember deepening the kiss, or encouraging him to deepen it, yet it deepened. She had no conscious awareness of time passing as they stood together in her kitchen, locked in this incredible embrace, yet time must have passed, for when they finally separated, she looked up to see three sets of wide eyes staring at them from the hallway.

"Mom?" Lydia asked, her tone incredulous.

"Daddy?" Marcie said, stunned.

"I told you," Danny said triumphantly. "I told you they were kissing."

"Wow," Lydia said, while Marcie still stared.

Max turned Cretia slightly to give her a screen from prying young eyes while she recovered her composure. "I think I'd better be going," he said. It pleased her to hear the slight tremor in his voice.

"I think maybe you should," she answered, not sure of her own voice.

"We're going to have to talk," he said, still steadying her in his arms.

"I know," she said. "Later."

"Later," he agreed. "You okay?"

"No," she said, smiling at him. "Are you?"

"Not at all," he agreed. "See you soon."

She nodded. "Soon."

He turned away from her. "Come on, Marcie. It's time to go." She watched them leave, wondering how she was going to satisfy the curiosity of her own two young starers.

Cretia usually did her shopping for the week on Saturday afternoons, so when Max called on Saturday and said he needed to do some shopping and would she mind coming along, she quickly left Danny and Lydia to their own devices and met him at her favorite grocery store. The moment she saw him, it was as if the last fifteen hours simply hadn't happened. She felt as flushed and breathless, and as eager to be in his arms, as she had been the last time they were together. *You're going to have to control yourself*, she warned herself firmly. *The man is going to think you're some kind of maniac.*

"Do you think we can talk quietly over a grocery cart?" he asked as he steered one into the aisle, Cretia walking beside him.

I doubt it, she thought, then she spoke wryly, "I don't know, but I have a hunch this is a safer place for this conversation than my kitchen would be."

"I know what you mean," he said. "Any place public is safer than any place private."

"Exactly." She flashed a smile.

He took her hand and placed it under his own on the cart handle. Looking ahead, as if at the rows of soup cans in front of him, he said, "If it weren't for this wild attraction I feel whenever I'm around you—"

"Wild attraction?" she asked, knowing that he must feel it just as she did, but awed to hear him say it.

"Since the first time I ever saw you, standing by the roadside next to that old clunker of yours."

"Before you even knew who I was?" Her sense of awe grew the more Max said.

"Before I'd ever heard your name," Max agreed, "and judging from the way you kissed me last night, I have to assume you feel something as well."

He was asking a lot, but he'd been honest with her. She nodded. "Much more than I want to admit to. I haven't been this attracted to anyone since my divorce."

He turned, looking her fully in the face. "Really?" She nodded. "I haven't, either." He shook his head. "Not since my divorce, I mean, and my divorce was almost twelve years ago."

"Mine's been more than six," Cretia answered.

"Wow," Max said, sounding much as Danny had last night. "So we really do have a situation on our hands, don't we?"

Cretia walked quietly beside Max for a moment, then said, "We could try just ignoring it."

He stopped the cart and gave her a long, searching look. "We could try," he said, "but I don't think I'd have much luck."

She smiled. "Me, either."

"So what if we agreed to spend some time together, have some fun, enjoy a little summer romance, but keep it light?" He gave her that beseeching look again, and she thought how dear, how sweet he looked.

"Light," she repeated, "like no strings, no commitments . . ."

"And nothing much heavier than a good, go-for-broke kiss like that one in your kitchen last night." He paused. "And that only every now and then when I simply can't stand to stay away from you any longer."

"Or I can't," she said. "Stay away from you, I mean."

He raised an eyebrow. "That's a possibility I hadn't considered."

"Well, don't think too much about it." She patted his hand and he chuckled. For a moment they just walked, looking at the shelves.

"So what do you think?" Max asked. "Do you think we can see each other occasionally, take the kids some places together, maybe go out together just the two of us now and then, only keep it—"

"Light?" She nodded. "I think it's worth a try."

"Me, too," he said. He shook himself, as if just waking from a dream. "Well, now that's decided, maybe it's time to get some shopping done."

Not until then had she realized their shopping cart was empty. "Okay," she agreed. "Shopping time." They went back to the first aisle and began again. This time they actually put groceries in the cart.

"Mom, do you think you might ever get married again?"

Cretia caught her breath and composed herself before turning to face her daughter. It was Sunday evening, two full days since their kids had interrupted the kiss in the kitchen. Cretia had thought of mentioning that moment to her children, putting fears to rest, stopping speculation, but unable to think of exactly what to say, she had avoided the subject instead. It seemed her children had, too—at least, until now.

"It's possible," she answered, "though it doesn't seem likely."

"Do you think you might marry Daddy again?"

That was a question Cretia hadn't prepared for, *though I should have*, she suddenly realized. Everything she heard or read about children of divorce said they always wanted their parents to get back together. She licked her lips, then looked her daughter squarely in the eye. "I don't think so, honey."

"I didn't think so, either." Lydia looked at the floor. She suddenly seemed fascinated with the pattern in the linoleum. She watched herself follow that pattern with her toe. "I was wondering . . . if you don't think you might get back together with Daddy, do you think you might marry Marcie's dad someday?"

Whew! Kids don't pull punches, do they? Cretia thought. Steadying herself with a deep breath, she said, "You know the Carmodys are only here for the summer, sweetheart. In August, they're going back to California, and Marcie will go back to live with her mother."

"We could go to California, too," Lydia said, "and maybe Marcie's mom would let her stay with us if we lived real close to where she is."

Cretia didn't want to think about that possibility. It was too distant, too remote, too frightening even to contemplate. *You need to remember it's Marcie she wants to keep, not Max*, she reminded herself. She decided to go with that tactic. "You've really gotten to be good friends with Marcie, haven't you, hon?"

"Yeah. We're pretty good buddies and all. Danny even likes her."

"I'm glad you're able to enjoy her company this much."

"It's the first time I ever thought about having a sister," Lydia admitted.

"That's something I never had," Cretia said, going to her daughter, putting an arm around her. "I always thought it would be great, but I got brothers instead."

"Uncle Joe and Uncle Mike." Lydia cuddled close.

Cretia realized how unsettling it must be for a child Lydia's age to see her mother kissing another man—anyone other than her father. *What must it be like to know your whole life could be changed overnight by a decision someone else makes for you?* she wondered, imagining what must have been going through Lydia's mind these past two days. She hugged her daughter even tighter. "That's right," she said. "Uncle Joe and Uncle Mike. They were pretty great brothers—"

"Even if they did torment you mercilessly," Lydia said with a twinkle, using the phrase Cretia had often used to describe her family relationships.

"Even though they did torment me mercilessly," she agreed, ruffling her daughter's hair. "But it would have been different to have a sister, I agree." She paused, letting the ideas they'd stirred up settle around them. "Having good friends can be a pretty good thing, too, you know, and you and Marcie can write letters once she's back in California, maybe even make phone calls on special occasions."

"Do you think?" Lydia said, looking hopeful for the first time since Cretia had quashed her hopes of a ready-made family.

"I think so," Cretia answered. "It's even possible you can visit each other again from time to time. You know, your Uncle Joe lives in southern California now, not too far from where Marcie lives with her mom."

"Really?"

She nodded. "Really. I'll bet it's less than an hour's drive from Uncle Joe's place to where Marcie's mom lives, even in heavy traffic."

"So we might be able to go see her?"

"No promises," Cretia pointed out. "It's a long way and it would cost money. We certainly couldn't make it in our old car! But who knows? In time, I expect we might be able to get out there for a visit, and Marcie might come back here to see you, too."

"Cool," Lydia said, smiling. Then slowly, the smile faded. "Mom?"

"Yes, hon."

"If you decided you wanted to get married again, would you let me and Danny have a vote about it?"

Careful with this one, Cretia, her inner voice warned. *You may someday have to live with whatever you say here.* She chose her words deliberately. "If I decided to get married again, I'd be the one making a lifetime commitment, so I'd be the one to make the choice." She saw Lydia's face fall and hurried on. "Of course, I'd want to know what you and Danny thought, so I'd be sure to ask your advice, but when it came right down to crunch time, I'd have to make that final decision for myself."

Lydia seemed to consider that for a moment before saying, "That seems fair."

Cretia breathed a shallow sigh.

"Mom?

"Yes, baby?"

"Really, now that you think about it, do you think you might ever get married again?"

It's time to alleviate some fears here, Cretia decided, putting other considerations to rest. "As I said, it's a possibility," she began, "but I think it's about as likely as . . ." She suddenly remembered an earlier comparison she had used with herself. "It's about as likely as finding a rainbow in the dark," she said.

Lydia grinned. "You don't see rainbows in the dark, Mom."

"Nope, you don't," Cretia agreed. "Nevertheless, I think it's just about that likely that I'll be getting married any time soon."

"Mom?"

One more time, Cretia thought. "Yes, honey?"

"I hope you do . . . someday. I mean, I hope you find someone who makes you really happy."

Cretia hugged her daughter against her, blinking back tender tears. "Thanks, sweetie," she said. "I appreciate that."

Chapter Five

It was Sunday, twelve days before Chris McAllister and Sarah Richards were to be married on the Fourth of July, and the McAllister family was consolidating resources. Even the traditional Sunday afternoon sing-along had been postponed so the family might spend the time organizing.

"Thanks for coming, everyone," Kate said when the table was finally cleared and she called her family to order. "Chris and Sarah have asked me to act as their wedding coordinator, and I'm going to need everybody's help to pull this off smoothly." Max was both surprised and pleased when she turned directly to him. "Max, Marcie, it's good of you to join us."

"Thank you for including us," Max answered. "With your permission, we'd like to consider ourselves honorary McAllisters for this summer."

There was a round of spontaneous applause and someone whistled. Max nodded acknowledgment on behalf of himself and his daughter, amazed to realize how good it felt, just to feel like family.

"As you can see, we are happy to include you," answered Kate McAllister Richards, mother of the groom and

82

stepmother to the bride. "Now when Wiley and I were married here . . ." She went on, reminding the family of how the most recent family wedding had been organized and involving the talents of different family members in planning for the next one, frequently flashing shy smiles at her new husband and gracefully deferring to the bride and groom in matters of judgment or taste.

Max listened briefly, then let his thoughts drift. As usual, they drifted quickly to Lucretia. In the week since their chat in the grocery store, he had spent as much time with her as he could arrange. They had shared meals together, taken their kids to the park together, listened to lots of music together—he had learned that she, like him, had a passion for Mozart—even cleaned up a messy flood together when the plumbing in her hall bathroom backed up and overflowed. For Max, no amount of time was ever enough. *She's really something, isn't she?* he asked himself, still brimming with pride over the fact that she chose to be with him and not with some slick younger man, someone like Logan Redhorse.

"Logan volunteered to pick up the folding chairs at the church," Chris spoke up in response to a question from his mother. "He'll get them here Thursday afternoon." Kate marked that item off her list, and Max let his lip curl in mild amusement. *Speak of the devil*, he thought.

But Logan wasn't any kind of devil. He had stopped by D. J.'s garage at least twice since he'd helped Max unload Cretia's engine, and each time he'd behaved like an old friend. In fact, the longer Max was around Logan, the more he was coming to like him. Still, it galled him to remember that when he left for California at summer's end, Cretia would still be here, and so would the attractive Navajo attorney.

"Now, I've made arrangements for the wedding cake—" Kate began.

"Again with your permission," Max cut in, volunteering as he'd been asked to do, "Cretia Sherwood would like to make the wedding cake as her gift to the newlyweds."

That brought another round of applause from everyone in the room. "Please tell Cretia we'd be delighted," Sarah answered. "Her cakes are the talk of the town."

He nodded, promising to carry the message back to Cretia as Kate checked another item off her planning list. He wouldn't even have known about Cretia's gifts as a baker if he hadn't mentioned he was coming to this planning meeting when he'd seen her yesterday afternoon. "I was planning to call them to offer it," she had told him. "Since you're going to be there, could you make the offer for me?" It hadn't surprised him that she'd offered to bake a cake. That she was so well known as a designer of specialty cakes was something else again. It served as further evidence that this woman who intrigued him was something very special.

"Very special indeed," he whispered aloud.

Marcie, seated at his elbow, looked up when he spoke. "What'd you say, Dad?"

"Nothing, honey." He tried to stay focused for a few minutes then, but he found himself remembering the plans he and Cretia had made to "keep it light." What a struggle that was coming to be! The more he was around Cretia— the more he saw her in early mornings or late nights, or even in the early evening when she had just finished a long workday and should have been exhausted and a wreck— the more he was persuaded that she had to be one of the most naturally beautiful women he'd ever known, and one of the most desirable.

I swear, you could dress that woman in burlap and pour a bucket of water over her head, and she'd still be lovely. I've never seen her when she wasn't. He spent the next few moments remembering how she had looked at various times during that week, even Tuesday night when she was angry with young Danny for deliberately annoying his sister, or Friday evening when she was perturbed with him for arriving half an hour late to the gourmet dinner she had prepared for just the two of them. Even last Thursday evening, when she'd had a near-sleepless night the night before, had put in a ten-hour day shooting tape on the reservation, and then come home to find the plumbing in the hall bathroom plugged and had pumped it herself with a hand plunger— even then she had looked like an angel, albeit a tired one. *Face it, Carmody*, he solemnly advised himself. *You're already half in love with her, and right on the verge of falling the rest of the way.*

"And you, Max?" Kate was saying.

"Uh . . . yes, ma'am?" Max had the odd sensation he'd been caught daydreaming in class.

"Do you think you could come over early Friday morning to help set up the last of the tables and chairs?"

"I'd be delighted," he answered, genuinely pleased to be included. "Is there anything else I can do?"

Kate ran down her list, quickly looking for anything that had gone unchecked. "It looks like we have all the bases covered, but I'll call on you if we need you as backup for anything. That is, if you don't mind."

"I hope you will," Max answered.

"It looks like we're all set then," Kate responded, concluding the meeting. The family members began to mill about while Max and Marcie excused themselves, starting for his red convertible.

"You know, Dad," Marcella began as she slid into the passenger seat beside him. "I was the maid of honor when Mom married Carl."

"I remember," Max said, only half listening as he started the car. The other half of his mind was already anticipating seeing Cretia.

"Now Sarah wants me to serve wedding cake at her wedding," Marcie went on.

"Yes," Max said. "I heard."

"I think that's kinda neat. I mean, I don't even know Sarah all that well, and she wants me to be in her wedding."

"Um-hm."

"Daddy?"

"Yes, Marcie."

"Do you think I'll get to be in your wedding when you get married again?"

Max was immediately grateful that he wasn't going very fast. At speed, he probably would have rolled the car. As it was, he fishtailed slightly in the gravel of the McAllisters' long driveway and very nearly choked on his own tongue before he was able to get the car pulled over to the side of the road. Finally settled, he tried to regain his calm. "Marcie, what makes you think I'm getting married again?"

"Seems like everybody does, eventually."

It was then that Max finally noticed the forlorn expression his daughter wore. He hesitated before saying anything, remembering a conversation he and Cretia had had earlier in the week about a similar talk she'd had with Lydia. It took little perceptiveness to realize that Marcella was watching her life change around her, and seeing little opportunity for herself—not quite a child anymore, but helpless compared to the adults around her—to influence those changes. His heart reached out, and his arms quickly followed.

"Come here, honey," he said, managing a hug, though it wasn't easy around the gearshift console. Into his daughter's ear, he whispered, "Are you worried about what will happen to you if I decide to remarry someday?"

"Well . . . I, uh, I just want to know . . . Where will I live, Dad? I mean, if you get married again."

"Oh, Marcie." He held her close, patting her back. The thought flitted through his mind that only a couple of weeks ago he had been wondering whether he could tolerate this child all summer. Now he found himself wondering how he could let her go when summer ended. "You know you'll always be my girl, no matter what else happens."

"Yeah, I know, but Dad?"

"What, honey?"

"Mom always said she loved me, too, then she married Carl, and well, Carl and me, we don't get along very well."

"I know, honey," Max sympathized. Though he wanted to see Joanna happy, he really wasn't all that crazy about Carl himself. Oh, the guy was decent enough, if a little pompous sometimes, but—

"Dad?"

"Yeah, honey."

"I really like Cretia. I mean, if you wanted to marry her, I think we could all get along just great."

Max choked, coughed, gasped for breath. "Whoa, there, Marcie. Don't go marrying me off just yet."

"But you like Cretia. I know you do. And well, we all saw you kissing her that one time—"

That one time and barely since, darn it. "I know, hon, but that doesn't mean—"

"It's just, if you wanted to marry her, that would be really cool with me. Just in case you think maybe you might want to someday."

Max took a deep breath. Part of him wanted to jump in and assure his daughter that he had no plans to marry again. Not ever. Not anybody. Not at all. Still, another little voice warned that it was better not to build any fences that couldn't be taken down easily, should one change his mind about fences. "Listen, Marcie," he said gently. "If I decide to marry again, you'll be among the first to know. But, honey?''

"Yeah, Dad?''

"I'd say it's unlikely." He remembered the line Cretia had used to Lydia and told him about later. "In fact, it's just about as likely as you finding a rainbow in the dark."

Marcella grimaced. "A rainbow in the dark, Dad?''

"That's right, honey. You see a rainbow glowing in the night sky, it's a pretty good guess your dear old dad is thinking about getting married again, but until you see that, well . . . Let's just say you don't have to worry about it.''

"I'm not worried," Marcie answered, but she kept her head perched awkwardly on his shoulder as he started the car again.

The next Wednesday Max took Marcie to Cretia's house early and picked up Danny as he left.

"Wow, this is cool, Max," Danny said as they pulled away from his house. "I mean, it's really neat that you're going to let me work with you today.''

"Well, I promised I would if I could, and although I can't take you to the shop where I'm working, I figured there's no reason you can't come with me to sift through the old wrecks at the auto yard.''

"I just wanted to say thanks, that's all," Danny said. "What are we lookin' for, anyway?''

Max explained what he wanted: a couple of carburetors in good working condition so he could rebuild the one in Cretia's car, a few small random parts to help him make the engine run more smoothly, "and at least two or three more water pumps of the same kind as in your mom's car.''

"Water pumps?'' Danny wrinkled his nose. "I didn't think there was anything wrong with her water pump.''

"There isn't, other than the normal wear and tear you see on old parts," Max answered, "but I think I may have found a small design flaw that could be corrected—not just on this pump, but on most water pumps in general. It would make a new replacement part for Carmody Auto Parts to produce. And if it's better than the original parts most factories are using when they build these things, well . . ."

"It could be a real good product for you guys, huh?" Danny said, catching the picture.

"Exactly, partner," Max said, giving Danny a high five.

They worked at the wrecking yard for nearly three hours, and Max found Danny a highly useful helper. In fact, Danny spotted several of the small parts Max wanted and two of the three water pumps Max carried to the front office when they were ready to leave. Once Max showed him what he was looking for, it was a simple matter for the boy to spot it again.

"You're good at this, Danny," Max said as he paid for the parts they'd gathered and loaded them into his trunk. "You've got a good brain for mechanical things, and a good eye for spotting what I'm looking for."

"I told you, my dad's a mechanic," Danny answered. "Guess it runs in the blood."

"I guess so," Max answered, quietly thinking, *I hope some of the guy's other traits don't "run in the blood."*

"He's not really a bad guy, you know." Danny spoke hesitantly, as if he'd heard Max's thoughts. "My dad, I mean. He had a hard time when he was younger, and I know he wasn't very good to my mom sometimes, but well, he's not really a bad guy." He paused, then a hopeful look came over him as he said, "Maybe you'll get to meet him someday."

Max chewed the inside of his lip, wondering how to choose the right words. "I'm not sure that would be a good idea, Danny."

"I think you'd like him if you got to know him," Danny said.

"Hmm. Maybe," Max answered aloud. *Maybe if the sun and earth both stopped turning in their orbits and he was the only guy who knew how to get them started again*, he thought bitterly. *I think I know too much about Danny Sherwood, Sr., to ever want to meet him in person. He does have a couple of nice kids, though*, he quickly amended, adding aloud, "He sure got a great kid when he got you, Danny."

Danny actually blushed. "Gee, thanks, Max."

"Don't mention it," Max said, but his thoughts remained on Cretia's ex-husband, and they were grim indeed. As he pulled up in front of Cretia's house, he found himself hoping the guy would show up drunk and troublesome sometime while he was here. *I'd show him where to get off real fast*, he thought glumly. *I'd show him I can protect my—*

His what? When had he started thinking of Cretia as his? Frustrated, he slammed his palm into the dashboard, causing Danny to jump.

"You okay, Max?"

"Yeah. I just forgot something, that's all."

"Should we go back to the auto yard?"

"Nah. It'll be okay," Max answered. He didn't want to tell Danny that what he'd forgotten was his promise to himself not to get involved.

"Dump the carrots out right there, next to the sink. Good, that's it," Cretia directed. She wasn't sure whether Max would be more help or hindrance in her kitchen today, but he'd volunteered to help her bake the various layers that would make up Chris and Sarah's wedding cake, and Cretia was willing to give him a try. *At least it should make the day interesting*, she thought. *I haven't had Max in the kitchen with me since that night . . . since that kiss. . . . Whew! Better not concentrate on that!* Aloud she said,

"Good, now just begin washing them carefully, one at a time."

"One at a time?" Max asked. "That's going to take a while."

"Oh, and that's not all, Max," she added. "Scrub each one with this vegetable brush while you're at it. Since I'm not going to peel the carrots, I need to make sure the toughest parts of the skin are removed before we start grating them."

"Isn't it easier to just make carrot cake from a mix?" Max asked, still grumbling to himself about scrubbing every carrot.

"Easier, yes. Better? Definitely not."

"Perfectionists," he said, rolling his eyes in an exaggerated gesture.

Cretia chuckled despite herself as she set up her industrial-size mixer and prepared several large pans to go into the oven.

"Are you going to bake all those at once?" Max asked.

"Oh, no. I couldn't fit them all into the oven at once," she answered. "I figure this many cakes will take three batches, each baking for roughly an hour at a time. Then after the first batch has cooled, I can take those layers out of the pans and fill those pans again for a fourth batch, then refill these for a fifth. Altogether, that should be enough carrot cake to make a four-tiered base with two small tiers on the top, above the pillars, and two double-layered side cakes."

"There'll be cake here to feed the Sixth Army," Max observed.

"I hope there'll be enough to feed two hundred guests," she answered.

"Two hundred?"

"A conservative estimate, I'd say. Both families are well known in this town and surrounding communities. They've sent out over three hundred invitations, but what with it being a holiday, they don't expect everyone to come. They're betting on fewer than half the invitations bringing in people, with some of those bringing more than one. But I think they're betting low. I wouldn't be surprised if we have three to four hundred there.''

"Kate wasn't counting on that many in her plans,'' Max said. Cretia thought he looked worried.

"Don't worry. If I know Kate, she has at least fifteen backup plans. She's the one who told me to be prepared in case they had lots more people than they planned on. In a pinch, we can cut the pieces smaller and feed at least three hundred fifty people with the cakes I'm making today.''

"No wonder it's an all-day project.''

"No wonder indeed. That's why I scheduled it for Saturday.'' She began the process of cracking and separating three dozen eggs. "And by the way, thanks for thinking of taking the kids to the park. They'll have a lot more fun there than here. It was a good idea.'' *I'm not really so sure of that. I suspect I'm going to need the chaperons myself.*

"Oh, I'm not sure,'' Max said, and she wondered if he was thinking the same thing she was. "They could have scrubbed carrots.''

Relieved, and amused by his grumpy look, Cretia laughed aloud.

"You've got a lot of eggs there,'' Max said after a while. "How come you have to separate each one like that?''

"I whip the egg whites separately before adding them into the batter,'' she explained. "It makes the cakes lighter.''

"Is it really worth all this trouble?'' Max didn't seem too sure.

"To me it is,'' she answered.

"Hmm.'' Max seemed noncommittal.

It was a few minutes later when she asked him to grate

the carrots for her and pulled out a rotary hand grater that his doubts created conflict. ''If you'll put on that small grating head, you'll get a nice, smooth, even bit of carrot that will make a light, fluffy batter,'' she said.

''Why not just put on this big one, grate them fast, and be done with it?'' he asked, putting on the larger-size head.

Cretia bit her lip, then acted as if changing the subject. ''You remember when you took Danny to the wrecking yard with you last week?'' she asked. ''You were looking for a certain kind of water pump, right? One with a little ridge on it?''

''That's right,'' he answered. ''Danny must have described it well.''

''Yes, he did,'' she said. ''Why didn't you just settle for just any old water pump you could get your hands on? They're all basically the same, right?''

''Basically, I suppose, but when you're looking for quality, details count.''

She grinned, gesturing toward the grater head. ''Exactly,'' she said.

''Oh,'' Max answered. She was pleased to see him changing the grater head, putting on the smaller one as she had asked.

For a while they worked companionably in silence. Then Max said, ''Did I tell you about my chat with Marcie last Sunday?''

''Just that you had the same talk with her that I had with Lydia the week before.''

''Yes, it was basically the same talk. Did I tell you she thought it would be 'cool' with her if I wanted to marry you?''

Marry me! Cretia found that thought didn't create the panic it might once have. Still, she decided to focus on the message about Marcie instead. ''She's a sweetheart. I like your little girl a lot.'' Then she looked away from him as she asked, ''What'd you tell her?''

''About getting married, you mean?''

She wondered if he was deliberately egging her on. ''Yes, about that.''

''I told her the same thing you told Lydia, that if she found a rainbow in a night sky, she'd know I was thinking about getting married again.''

Cretia chuckled. ''Imagine the two of them, looking for night rainbows.''

Max didn't smile at the image. Instead he came around the counter so he stood beside her and put his hand on her shoulder. ''Don't you think it's kind of cute, the two of them trying to get us together?''

Cretia looked into his eyes. The expression there took her breath away. ''Max, I think you need to get back to grating carrots.''

''You know, I can't help but think of how we have this whole house to ourselves, for the rest of the whole day.''

She felt her breath coming faster. She dropped her eyes, unwilling to meet his. ''That's temptation speaking, Max. Tell it to go away and leave you alone.''

''Is that what you want me to do?''

''Trick question,'' she said, easing away from him. ''What I want may not be what I think is best—for both of us.'' Ducking under his arm, she put the large counter between them.

He chuckled, though there was a hollow sound in it. ''Okay, I get the message, but Cretia?''

''Yes, Max?''

''If I'm a very good boy and I grate my carrots like I'm supposed to, do you think I can talk you into one more great kiss like that last one we shared in this kitchen? Maybe sometime later today?''

She finally felt able to meet his eyes. "I'll look forward to it," she said.

He nodded, his expression still filled with that same intensity. "So will I," he answered, the look in his eyes a promise.

They stood in the kitchen surrounded by cakes. It had been seven hours since they had put the first batch in the oven and now the counters were covered in cake—different layers, different shapes, all of them smelling deliciously of carrots, sugar, and cinnamon.

"Thanks, Max," Cretia said as she pulled out a huge roll of aluminum foil and began the process of wrapping each layer, preparing them to go into the second fridge she kept in the garage, just for this purpose. "You really were a help today, and I appreciate it."

Max came around the counter and took the roll of aluminum foil from her hands. "So do I get my reward?" he asked. He was giving her that look again, and Cretia felt instantly breathless.

"You know," she answered honestly, "part of me has been hoping you'd forget all about that promise."

"And the other parts?" he goaded, running his hand along her bare upper arm until she quivered beneath his touch.

"I haven't been giving them a vote," she answered.

Max chuckled, then sobered, drawing her against him. "Have I told you how beautiful you are?" he said.

"Beautiful?" She couldn't help feeling shocked. After all her years of feeling dowdy, even homely . . . "Me? Beautiful?"

"What? Did you want to hear it again?" Max's voice was practically purring. "You're beautiful, Lucretia," he said, kissing her hair. "You're probably the most beautiful woman I've ever known."

"Max, I don't—"

"Shhh," he said, kissing her lips in a whisper-soft gesture designed simply to quiet her. "You have the glossiest, near-black hair, and the most perfect skin, especially right here," he said, kissing her neck.

"Ummmm." She thought she might be melting. "Max, I—"

"And your eyes," he said, continuing his speech and gently kissing her temples beside each eye as he spoke. "You have beautiful eyes, too, large and soft and deep. I feel like I could fall right into those eyes. And you smell absolutely delicious, like orange blossoms and honeysuckle. You always have."

She sighed. "Max. Oh, Max—"

"Yes, love," he whispered. "What is it you want to say?"

"I can't remember," she murmured, going limp in his arms, giving him a lazy, dreamy smile. Somewhere along the way she had decided to stop fighting her fears and simply trust him. Hadn't he promised he wouldn't ask anything of her that she was unwilling to give? And didn't he seem to be one man she really could trust? He'd always proven trustworthy so far.

"Kiss me, Cretia," he finally said, and she complied, melting against him, giving herself up to the sensations, the intensity, to him.

It seemed like a long time later when they both surfaced, gasping for air. The look on Max's face was like nothing she'd ever seen before. He looked stunned, amazed, almost frightened.

"Max," she murmured, unable to manage anything but his name.

"Wow," he said in answer, his breathing still ragged.

"Max, I—" She paused again, unable to say the things

she felt like saying, to tell him how she felt, what she'd decided.

He shifted away from her, that deer-in-the-headlights look still on his face. Still breathless, he glanced at his watch. "Almost five," he said unevenly. "I told the kids I'd pick them up at five o'clock."

Cretia felt the stab of disappointment. It surprised her, since she hadn't expected it. "Then maybe you'd better hurry," she said, her heart not quite in her words. "I'll get the cakes wrapped and put away while you're gone."

"Okay," he answered. He glanced around her kitchen. "That's quite a day's work we've done here, isn't it?"

"Yes," she said. "Quite."

"Cretia?" He paused at the doorway.

"Um-hm?"

"You've spent the whole day in the kitchen. Don't cook tonight. Let me bring home chicken and fixings. We can spread a blanket on the grass and picnic in the backyard."

She nodded. "Okay, this is a good day for that."

"Remember, I promised I'd get your kids some burgers or greasy chicken sometime before the summer was over."

"Yes, I remember," she said.

"And Cretia?"

She smiled. "Yes, Max?"

"I always keep my promises." The sizzling look he gave her then almost melted her right to her toes. "That's the only reason I'm leaving now."

She took a long moment to read his eyes, to see the whole message waiting for her there. It both lifted her heart and made it race like an overfueled engine. "Thank you," she whispered.

He saluted as he went out the door.

Max stumbled down the hallway, rubbing sleep from his eyes as he found his way to the family room where he could hear sounds. Since Meg and Jim had gone to the McAllister family home as usual, he knew the noise must be Marcie. When he'd crawled home exhausted after church, then elected to skip the family dinner and planning meeting on the grounds that he'd worn himself to a frazzle yesterday— first in the kitchen with Cretia, then working late on some schematics for Nate at the plant—Marcie had chosen to stay, too. "Just to keep you company, Dad," she'd said.

He smiled. *Marcie keeping me company. Who would have thought?*

He stepped into the family room to find her draped across an overstuffed chair, tossing kernels of popped corn at her mouth and dodging to catch them. The evidence scattered around her on the floor suggested she wasn't very skilled at it. "Hi," she said, beaming as he walked in.

The warm tug in the center of his chest practically dragged the smile out of him. He stifled the reprimand that had occurred to him when he saw her popcorn mess. "Hi," he answered instead. "Whatcha watchin'?"

"Just some music videos." She pointed to the couch. "Join me?"

Music videos? Max's lip curled in distaste; this was nothing like Mozart. "Nah, I . . ." He saw the look of disappointment flit across her face, disappearing almost as quickly as it came. "Well, I don't have to go anywhere for a while. Maybe I'll sit for a minute, if you don't mind."

"Sure."

He sat on the couch, trying not to fidget as he listened to the repetitive, mindless lyrics. He couldn't help himself. "Dah, dah, dah? That's a lyric?"

"Ah, come on, Dad," Marcie said, refusing to take the bait. "You're not hearing the whole thing. There's some really neat stuff in the verses."

"But that's the chorus?"

She stood, smiling like some beneficent angel. "Don't

be too mean about the lyrics, Daddy,'' she said, coming close to sit next to him. "You forget. Mom's new husband listens to the oldies station, so I've heard silly songs about disco-dancing ducks and polka-dot bikinis. My generation hasn't come up with anything dumber than that.'' She grinned and sat beside him.

"Yeah, well, you've got a point there."

"Of course I do.'' While Max sat uncomfortably, uncertain what to do, a rather smug-looking Marcie lifted his arm, snuggled in against him, then settled his arm around her shoulders. She set her bowl on his lap. "Want some popcorn?"

"Uh, no thanks."

"Okay,'' she said, snuggling closer and aiming a kernel at her mouth.

"Uh, Marce?"

"Yeah, Daddy?"

"Do you think maybe you could *put* the kernels in your mouth instead of throwing them? Just for the sake of the carpet, you understand."

She looked around. "It does look pretty bad, doesn't it?"

"Well . . .'' He shrugged.

"Don't worry, Daddy. I'll clean up.'' She sighed and snuggled into his chest. Suddenly Max felt happier, stronger, and more capable than he'd ever felt in his life.

On Monday afternoon, Cretia came home a little early to take the girls shopping. Sarah had called the wedding "fairly informal'' and had insisted they just wear "nice Sunday dresses'' from their own closets, rather than spending any money on new clothing just for the wedding. Still, they both wanted something new to wear, and they had become so close, almost like sisters. To Cretia, it seemed important that they have something nice, maybe matching.

She had begged a swatch of the violet fabric from the dress Sarah was having made for her maid of honor—her best friend, Eden. Maybe if they were lucky, she could come close to matching the color.

Max was at the house when she arrived and she explained to him what she had in mind. "Great idea," he said, digging in his pocket to come out with his wallet. "How much do you think you'll need?"

"You don't need to do this, Max," she said, waving his money away. "You've done so much for us already. Let me get the dresses for the girls."

"Nonsense," he said. "You feed us here a lot of the time, and you've had Marcie at your place almost every day for the past month. Besides, I can buy my own daughter's dresses." He handed her a hundred-dollar bill. "Wait! They'll need shoes, too, won't they?" He counted off another hundred, then a third. "Get matching things for both of them, why don't you? And maybe get something for yourself? Maybe a new shirt for Danny?" He reached for another hundred.

"Max, for heaven's sake!" Cretia backed away before he could hand her the whole wallet. "I'm just getting a couple of simple dresses." She tried to hand the money back to him.

"Nah, keep it," he said. "Get whatever you need or want. If there's anything left when you get back, you can hand me the change."

She looked at him, already putting his wallet away, and at the wad of cash in her hand. She thought how many times over the last years this much extra money would have been enough to ease her financial worries for a month or more. It reminded her, too strongly, of the differences between them. "All right, Max," she answered. "I'll be sure to bring most of it back."

The look on her face must have reached him. He caught her hand. "Really, Cretia. Spend as much as you like. If you need more than that—"

"No, Max. We won't need more than that."

"Okay then. Spend as much of it as you need or want to spend." He seemed to need to say something to cheer her. "I faxed the specs for the new water pump design to the plant this morning. Nate, my production manager, has some guys working on a prototype already. I wouldn't be surprised if it does very well for us. So you see, I owe—"

"You owe me nothing, Max." She stiffened her spine. "But on behalf of the girls, I appreciate your generosity. I'll try to see they get some nice things."

"Cretia, I—" He reached for her hand.

She slipped away. "We'll see you later," she said, calling to Lydia and Marcie as she left by the kitchen door.

As he watched them drive away, Max stood wondering how he had offended her, and pondering at how easily it seemed to happen.

Rainbow Productions closed its office at five o'clock on Wednesday, so the four people who worked there—Meg, Kurt, and Cretia all full-time and Alexa part-time—could all have Thursday to get ready for the Big Event. Cretia had argued that they should keep the office open on Thursday to receive orders. She'd continued arguing right up until Meg told her she could take the day as paid "comp" time in exchange for the extra hours of work she'd put in since she'd started working as a field producer, shooting tape on the reservation for their new program. It was tentatively titled *The Weaver's Wage,* a sequel to their award-winning documentary, *The Weaver's Way.* Cretia had suggested the name. Her bosses seemed more and more pleased with her all the time, and the raise she had received with her latest promotion made her feel like she had a little extra cash to spend for the first time in her life.

Maybe that's why I was so put off by Max giving me money the other day, she thought Thursday morning as she set up her little sewing machine on the dining room table. The girls' lilac-colored dresses both fit fairly well, but with a few simple alterations, they'd look smashing. She had already measured and fitted the girls; now it was a simple matter to alter the dresses.

She was hard at work extending the darts on Marcie's dress, making it a little less full, when Max pulled up, knocked briefly at the kitchen door, then let himself in.

"Sewing now?" he asked. "Is there nothing you can't do?"

"I guess that remains to be seen," Cretia answered coolly. She hadn't quite forgiven Max for flashing his money at her.

"Where are the kids?" he asked, looking around.

"Their dad took the day off today to spend with them, since they're going to be at the wedding all day tomorrow."

"That was good of him," Max said, trying for an even, neutral tone.

"Where's Marcie?" she asked, finally noticing that his daughter wasn't with him.

"She went out to the McAllister house with Meg. Said she thought she could help set up."

"Oh." She looked around for an excuse to send him away. She just didn't need this complication today, when she already had more than enough to do. "How come you're not working on car parts?"

"The guy who owns the garage where I'm working took the day off. He'll be closed up till Monday."

"Oh. Guess that's a good reason not to work there."

"Yeah." He stood quietly, watching as she made careful

seams, trimming away the extra fabric. "You seem to know what you're doing."

"Yeah. I guess I do. You need to understand, Max. I've been taking in oversized clothes or cutting things down to new sizes since I was—"

"Cretia, I didn't mean to offend you by offering you money. I wasn't even really offering the money to you," he said, blurting it out. He looked so uncomfortable, she almost felt sorry for him. Almost. "I'm sorry, Cretia. I'm really sorry. I just didn't realize how it would come across to you. I really didn't mean to suggest you couldn't afford to do it yourself. It was just my way of trying to help with the wedding preparations. I didn't mean—"

She kissed him. At the moment, it seemed the only way to stop him from embarrassing himself even further.

"What—?" he said, breaking the kiss.

She cut him off with another kiss. This one lasted longer. This one had some of the force of the anger she had felt, though somehow it came across as something different in the process of moving from her mind to her lips.

"How—?" he started again.

She sighed. How could she explain to him how he made her feel when he bought a car for her, or gave her money to buy a dress for her own child? In that instant, she decided she couldn't explain, not in any way that a man who had always had money could understand, and that it probably didn't matter that much, anyway.

"Cretia?" he asked, his face a mask of confusion.

"Oh, shut up and kiss me," she answered.

Not surprisingly, he did.

Chapter Six

Max yanked a tissue from his shirt pocket and wiped at his forehead, then glanced at his wristwatch. It was not yet ten, and already the July sun was turning the high desert into an oven—a very *noisy* oven. It seemed the noise had been growing exponentially since about seven-thirty this morning, when he'd first arrived to help the family set up tables and chairs. Though most of the setup had been finished yesterday, there were still last-minute arrangements to be made, like putting up the tables in the shade where Cretia—lovely in her soft, lavender-blue silk shift—was busy now, preparing the space for the wedding cake, or setting up another hundred chairs as the crowd continued to grow. Through it all, the noise level rose.

People milled, chatting and visiting; children ran in and out of the crowd, giggling and taunting one another; somewhere a viola was tuning to a piano in uncontrolled cacophony. Then the pianist and viola player got their act together and began Pachelbel's Canon in D. A hush rippled through the crowd as parents gathered their children and people found their places. There was something sobering and sacred about a wedding.

Max would have added a third "s": sobering, sacred, and scary. Terrifying, in fact. He found weddings frightening to the maximum. As a rule, he tried to miss them. Ever since his own debacle, he had found it uncomfortable to be in the presence of starry-eyed couples who were making commitments that no more than half of them would keep. At one particularly ill-timed gala, which he had been unable to avoid, he had actually heard the best man betting the bride's brother that it wouldn't last two years. As he recalled, that marriage hadn't made it to the first anniversary before falling apart in guilt and accusation.

Happily ever after just isn't much of a bet these days, Max told himself as he watched the guests gathering and the seats filling up. Then another little voice in the back of his head spoke up: *It doesn't have to be that way.*

There came Kate McAllister Richards, escorted on the arm of her son-in-law and taking the place reserved for the mother of the bride. From all accounts, she had enjoyed a wonderful marriage to Jim McAllister, father of the big, blond hunks who had grown up in this farmhouse. She had even remained loyal to his memory through many years of widowhood before Wiley Richards came along.

Wiley was a good example, too—widowed by his wife's death when Sarah was just a girl, faithful to her memory throughout many long, lonely adult years before finding Kate. With years of successful marriage already behind them, Kate and Wiley stood every chance of having a healthy, happy union. Then, in the next generation, Joan and Bob had recently celebrated a tenth anniversary, and from the way they'd looked whenever Max had seen them together, he surmised they had a long and happy life ahead of them. Young Jim had certainly been a blessing for his own half sister. He couldn't have imagined Meg as content, as joyful, as settled as she seemed right now.

Rounding out the family, Kurt and Alexa, though still

newlyweds, certainly gave every impression of being happy together, and the couple who were marrying today seemed like a good bet, too. *If I had to make a bet about Chris and Sarah's wedding*, Max admitted silently, *I'd bet it's going to last as long as both of them do.*

So maybe there's no reason to be so jaded about it, that second little voice was saying. *Look around you. There are lots of happy couples here.* Max looked, and he saw. His little voice was right; there were dozens of couples here who had already seen long years pass behind them, and who would be certain to go into the future prepared for the long haul. Armed with the shield of honorable commitment, they were equipped to fight off the kinds of problems that threatened or even destroyed other couples.

Maybe that's all it takes, he thought with more hope than he'd felt in some time. *Maybe couples can stay married just by promising themselves and each other that they will. Maybe they can even promise each other to be happy about the journey.*

Yes, maybe they can, Max thought, agreeing with his own inner voice. As he found his seat, and those he was saving for Cretia and the kids, he felt more hopeful than he had in some time. Amazed at himself, he found he was actually looking forward to this wedding, and possibly, to other weddings in the future. Maybe Marcie was right. Maybe the time was coming when he could think about marrying again.

The final strains of Pachelbel's Canon in D floated through the noisy crowd, quieting them and bringing people to their seats. Cretia finished placing the base she had set up for Chris and Sarah's giant wedding cake, looking distractedly at the growing numbers of guests. Many of them were in shorts and T-shirts, appropriate attire for the weather, if not for a wedding.

"If it gets much hotter, or the crowd gets much bigger, we're going to be in trouble with this cake," she mumbled, aware that her much-touted cream cheese icing was likely to be more like cream cheese soup if temperatures hit the mid-nineties just when they were planning to serve. One local forecaster had predicted that on her radio this morning and she had retaliated by turning the radio off. She didn't think that would help the cake much, though, if the icing turned to soup while the guests were waiting. "I guess we'll just have to do what we have to do," she said, thinking of the delicately frosted cake that now sat in sections in the second fridge Kate had loaned the newlyweds for that purpose, and which Chris had set up on his mud porch off the kitchen. "If worse comes to worst, I've brought extra toothpicks."

"Do you think the sun is going to melt the icing?" Lydia asked as she approached her mother. She looked as distracted and concerned as Cretia felt.

"I hope not, honey." Cretia tried for a reassuring smile. "If it does, we'll just have to do the best we can to save it."

"We don't usually do outdoor cakes," Lydia observed. The "we" made her mother smile. Lydia hadn't learned much about the baking yet, and she knew very little about decorating, but she was a veteran at helping put cakes together at the wedding or reception site, and she knew more clever ways to cut and serve a cake than most adult women had ever seen.

This year they had the blessing of additional help. Just behind Lydia, Marcie stood in her identical sleeveless lilac-colored shift, pacing and looking distractedly at the crowd. "Do you think there's going to be enough cake for everyone?" she asked.

"I think so," Cretia assured her. "The way I count, there are still under three hundred here, and it's almost time to begin."

"Then maybe we'd better go take our seats," Lydia said.

"Dad's holding places for us," Marcie added.

"Is Danny there, too?"

"He wasn't a minute ago," Lydia answered, "but I bumped into him when I was walking over and I told him to go sit by Max. I think he was headed that way when I came in."

"Great," said Cretia. "Let's go join them then."

She steered the girls toward Max and Danny, marveling as she did so at how comfortable it had become to have Marcie with them, almost as if she had always been a part of their family. *Careful, Cretia*, she warned herself. *You're getting into dangerous thinking again.* Then that dangerous thinking turned up to full alarm mode as she approached Max and her son, found them talking quietly and gesturing to one another, laughing conspiratorially over something one of them had said, and thought, *They look just like father and son.* That observation so stunned her that she was wide-eyed and wary when she settled next to Max, crossing her long legs at the ankle.

She looks stunning, positively marvelous, Max thought, his eyes on the shapely, long legs Cretia folded in front of her. *There isn't a woman here who can hold a candle to her.* With a touch of embarrassment, offset by unabashed pride, he realized he was engaging in some very possessive male thinking about this woman who was here with him. He wanted to stand up and crow to make everyone look and take notice. He wanted to shout, "Hands off, guys! She's with me!" Mostly he wanted to get her alone somewhere and show her just how possessive he felt.

Then another idea struck him. He wanted her to be his—for real, for always. If the heat weren't bad enough, that thought alone could have made him feel faint.

Leave it alone, Max, he warned. *You're just catching*

wedding fever, that's all. You know it's a highly communicable disease, so hang onto your sanity and maybe you'll stay immune. Just then Cretia looked up at him and smiled, those dark chocolate eyes glimmering under long, black lashes, and he wiped his brow again, suddenly pulsing with heat.

"I think I recognize the violist," Cretia whispered to Max, not sure he had heard her. "She was in Jim and Meg and Danny's class in high school."

"Hmm," Max said.

Taking that as a sign of disinterest, Cretia stood slightly to try to see better. She got a good look at the woman's face, confirming her first guess, but kept the dialogue to herself. *It is Angelica DeForest. I thought so. Gosh, is she still doing the same shtick she did in high school? After all these years?*

She remembered Angelica as the one senior too good for everyone else. Too superior to allow herself to be called "Angie," too highbrow to play popular music, too elite to sit with the regular crowd at games or assemblies, Angelica had been one of the few other kids at school who enjoyed classical music. But she had been way too good for a little freshman like Lucretia Vanetti, and had quickly rebuffed any efforts Cretia had made to get to know her. *Maybe that's why she's still Angelica DeForest after all these years. Maybe when you treat people like that, you deserve to be lonely.*

Cretia suddenly felt ashamed of herself. *That wasn't very nice of me. I'm not in any position to judge.* In the silence that followed as the canon came to a close, she heard that little voice answer, *No, Cretia, you're not.*

Then, as a few people in the crowd applauded the canon, Cretia noticed something that shocked her. Angelica De-Forest turned bright red at the show of appreciation, and ducked behind the piano, making a show of reaching for something in her viola case.

Or is she? Cretia wondered. *Is she making a show, the way I always thought? Or is she just hiding out because she's shy? That blush certainly looked like embarrassment. Maybe she plays the music because she loves it, but is embarrassed to have people watch her. Maybe that's why she seldom solos in church, but usually plays in situations like this, where the musicians are virtually invisible.* Then the shocker: *Oh, my! Maybe she was never stuckup or conceited or superior, the way we always believed she was. Maybe she was always just shy, too shy to know how to accept proffered friendship.* As she thought that, she suddenly remembered moments in high school when she had approached Angelica and been rebuffed, or thought she was. She had taken Angelica's mumbled responses as a show of disinterest, just as she had taken Max's response just now, *but wouldn't she have responded the same way if she had just been tongue-tied and unaware of what to say?*

Tears came unbidden to Cretia's eyes. *I've been unfair to you, Angelica DeForest*, she said in her heart. *Please forgive me.* Then determined to learn immediately from the lesson, she turned to Max and whispered, "I think I just learned something new about myself, Max. Did you realize I can be a real snob sometimes?"

"You? Never!" Max answered. Bless him. He actually looked surprised.

The violist began another number and Max recognized the opening strains of a Mozart serenade he had always liked. "Mozart," he whispered to Cretia. "The violist has good taste."

"Yes, she does," Cretia said, feeling a need to make recompense. "She always has."

They played only a few phrases of the serenade, just

enough to create a musical cue, allowing the minister, groom, and best man to come onto the front porch through the door to the front parlor. Max thought Chris looked especially nice today, decked out for his wedding. He looked nervous, all right, but more happy than nervous, and more eager than both. *He's getting a bride he really wants*, Max thought with a touch of envy, *one he knows well and is prepared to live with for the rest of his life. He has every right, every reason to be happy.*

Reverend Phelps took his place beneath the flowered archway the McAllister brothers had built and Logan took his place beside Chris. Max couldn't help noticing that Logan was looking pretty spiffy today, too, his dark slacks and gray, western-cut coat a nice contrast to the gleaming white worn by the groom. Max cast a speculative glance at Cretia, wondering if she'd noticed, but her gaze seemed riveted on the doorway, and he guessed she was waiting for the bride's entrance. Then the reverend nodded to the pianist, the musicians cut short the serenade, the wedding march began, and all eyes turned to await the bride.

Of course, it wasn't Sarah who entered first, but her maid of honor, a beautiful young woman Max had met briefly for a moment earlier today, when she had first come from the airport. He had recognized her loveliness even then, despite the rollers in her midnight-black hair and the look of near-panic on her face as she rushed to make up for a late flight. Now Eden was a vision in lavender-blue, the dress fitted through the top but sort of dreamy and floaty in the skirt, the color a near-perfect match for what Cretia wore. *If anyone here could compete with Lucretia, it might be Eden*, Max thought, allowing himself to admire the tall, slender beauty who took her place on the minister's other side and turned toward the door to await her friend. He looked from the stunning woman on the porch to the simply dressed one beside him and made his decision. *Even then, she'd run a close second. No one here is as beautiful as my Cretia.* He caught himself in the thought. *Not "my" or "mine." You've got to stop that, Max. Really, you must.*

Still his pride swelled almost to bursting at the thought that even a woman with Eden's rare beauty was eclipsed by Lucretia's loveliness. He found himself wanting to crow again. Instead he leaned and whispered into Cretia's ear, "Do you have any idea how truly lovely you are?"

Cretia blushed lightly, ducked her head, and whispered, "Shh. It's time to stand for the bride."

Sarah appeared at the door as she said it, and the audience stood, offering silent tribute to their Queen for a Day, the star of this celebration. Sarah stepped onto the porch, resplendent in a simple, mid-calf ivory gown. She wore a wreath of yellow rosebuds and white baby's breath in her red-gold hair, and in the small of her back, her lavender-blue ribboned sash tied in a stylish bow. She hesitated briefly while Wiley stepped up beside her, also looking stylish in his gray suit, then she took his elbow and they walked together the few steps that would take her to her new husband. Watching, Max thought she, too, was a lovely woman, and a happy one. She looked as eager for this ceremony as Chris was. Still he couldn't help thinking Cretia would look even lovelier in ivory satin. *Stop it, Max. Just cut it out!* he told himself firmly, but the image of Cretia in bridal satin remained.

The musicians ended the wedding march, the minister invited the audience to be seated, and the ceremony began. Reverend Phelps always kept his weddings short and simple. *That's just what I'd want if I were getting married again*, Cretia thought, then immediately banished the idea. *You had your chance, girl*, she told herself firmly. *Now any dream you ever had of "happily ever after" is long gone and far out of reach.*

But is that really so? her little voice asked. *Look at Sarah. She's only a little younger than you are, and she was married before.* Cretia wanted to argue with her little voice, to tell it angrily to mind its own business and leave her alone, but she couldn't help thinking that it had a point. She herself had attended a bridal shower after Sarah eloped with rodeo cowboy Jake McGill. At the time she was already three years married herself, and jaded enough to know that Sarah was likely to have it rough, married to a wild one like Jake. She didn't know what the quality of that marriage had been—she suspected few people did— but she knew Sarah seemed ever so much happier now than she ever had been with Jake "the Snake" McGill. Sarah had had her first chance, just as Cretia had. The one major difference was that Sarah had lost her husband to death, not divorce. As Sarah herself liked to put it, "A rodeo bull named Widowmaker decided to live up to his name," and Sarah had been a widow ever since.

At least, until Chris McAllister came along. Cretia watched Sarah take her vows with a small touch of envy. *Those McAllister men are really something*, she thought quietly. Then, giving Max a sideward glance, *Even their shirttail relatives have a certain raw charm.*

Ah, who am I kidding? She almost spoke the words aloud. *There's nothing raw about Max's charm. He's polished, distinguished, attractive, and as silver-tongued as they come. Goodness! The man could talk you into anything, if he were so inclined. Thank goodness he isn't that kind of man.* And he wasn't. She knew it the same way she knew she loved her children, trusted in it with the same assurance she felt about the sun coming up tomorrow morning. Max had a devilish charm and sophisticated style, but he was a good man, and she knew she could trust him with her safety, her children, maybe even with her heart. She was so sure of him that she thought she might even risk falling in love.

Now where did that thought come from? she asked herself, just as Sarah said, "I do." Her little voice answered, *Your heart, Lucretia. Listen to your heart.*

"I think we're in trouble here," Lydia said, watching the top half of the bottom cake layer slide slowly off the bottom half.

"Who knew we were going to have record high temperatures?" Cretia asked. She could feel tears of frustration beginning to build in the corners of her eyes, and she firmly ordered them to go away and leave her alone. *I have enough to worry about without sitting here bawling like a baby. Still, what am I going to do?* she thought with dismay. *The toothpicks I brought to hold this thing together are about as effective as trying to patch a breaking dam with chewing gum.*

"They're about ready for the cake out there," Max said as he came through the door.

"Well, we're not ready in here," Cretia snapped, then immediately relented. "I'm sorry, Max. I know the weather isn't your fault. It's just that all that time and effort we put into it already, and they're out there waiting for a beautiful cake, and I don't know what—" She stopped, her voice breaking.

"Hey, hey, it can't be that bad." Max took her into his arms, cradling her head against his hard chest, making her feel loved, cared for, cherished—the very words Chris and Sarah had just spoken to one another. "What's the problem? Anything I can help with?"

"It's the heat," Lydia said, covering for her mom. "The frosting keeps melting, and the cake parts just keep sliding all over the place."

"Um. That's a problem," Max agreed, still holding

Cretia against him. She ducked her head into the shallow of his shoulder, unwilling to come out and face the mess awaiting her on the McAllisters' kitchen table.

"How does your mother usually hold a cake together?" Max asked. Cretia thought it ironic that he addressed the question to Lydia with her standing right there, then she realized he was picking up on her own reluctance to face things, allowing her to disappear for a moment while he sheltered her. She wondered if anyone had ever done anything this kind for her before.

"Toothpicks," she whispered against his shoulder. "I hold it together with toothpicks. Only nobody makes toothpicks big enough to handle a catastrophe like this one."

Max paused, looking strangely thoughtful. "Maybe someone does," he said. He held her away from him so he could look into her eyes. "Cretia, Danny and I bought a kite kit earlier this week. We were going to build it this afternoon. It's got several feet of quarter-inch wooden dowelings in it."

"Doweling?" Cretia asked. She could feel hope rising.

"Major-sized toothpicks," Max translated, in case she had missed his thinking. "All I need now is a small hand-saw—"

"Or some pruning loppers?" Kurt McAllister asked from behind them. "We've got some in the toolshed."

"Great!" Max said. "Get them, will you? Cretia, I've got the kit in the trunk of my car. I'll be back in no time. You ladies go ahead and put together whatever else you need and we'll have that cake put together before you can sneeze."

"I think we just might," Cretia said, gathering strength from his enthusiasm. Then she rose quickly on her tiptoes to plant a short-lived but potent kiss on his mouth. "Thanks, Max. Thanks so much."

"No problem," he said, heading for the car.

"No kidding?" she heard Kurt say as he went out, following Max. "You and Cretia? How long has that been going on?" She only wished she could hear Max's answer.

The cake-cutting ceremony had gone without a hitch and Max watched with pride as Cretia, Lydia, and Marcie skillfully cut small slices of wedding cake, handing them out to the assembled guests. The whole crowd had applauded their appreciation when the cake had appeared on the scene, wheeled out on a kitchen cart and carefully slid into place on the platform Cretia had crafted for it in the shade of the dooryard sycamores. No one but a half-dozen people who had been with them for those few minutes in the kitchen knew it had taken some skilled engineering to put the thing together and to cause it to hold in the face of the day's high temperatures.

That and a few hastily mumbled prayers, Max thought, beaming at his ladies. His ladies. His. He was beginning to feel that way about all of them—Marcie, who was no longer the child his ex-wife had taken away with her, but who had somehow become his daughter and an essential part of his life; Cretia, who was quickly becoming as essential to his life as breathing, and just as hard to forget. Even Lydia was beginning to feel like one of his own. *Gosh, I'm even falling for Danny*, he half-mumbled to himself as he looked around to find the little boy playing with Joan and Bob's daughter, Alice, and a couple of other children he didn't recognize. *They're all beautiful people, wonderful people, people I'm happy and proud to know. They're beginning to feel like family to me.*

Family. Did he even dare think that word? *Don't get carried away with this wedding stuff, Max. Remember, it's like a fever, and you're unusually vulnerable to infection just now.* He thought of how Kurt McAllister, the groom's brother, had asked about his relationship with Cretia. He had laughed it off, answering that she was too wise to have much to do with him, but he'd been thinking about it. The angels in heaven only knew how much he'd been thinking about it! *Just don't get carried away, Max*, he warned again. *This isn't the sort of thing one can rush into.*

Just then the DJ the couple had brought in to spin some records for them announced a dance "for the bridal couple" and Chris took the microphone from him to announce that the best man and maid of honor should join them, then invited Kate and Wiley to join them, too. Max, together with the rest of the assembled audience, turned his attention to the dance area on the lawn to watch as Chris took his new bride into his arms and began a slow, gentle waltz around the green.

Chris and Sarah couldn't have looked happier. Their love for each other shone in their faces, and again Max had the happy feeling that here was one marriage that would last.

Then as he watched, Logan offered Eden his hand. *What?* Max observed with surprise. *Logan and Eden?* All this time he had thought of Logan as a rival for Cretia's attention, yet as he watched the look on Logan's face as he tenderly took Eden into his arms, there was no mistaking where Logan's attention lay. The man looked smitten if ever Max had seen a smitten man—and he had, once or twice at least, even in his own mirror. *Who would have guessed?* he wondered with awe as the second couple joined the first in a moment of sheer magic.

The DJ picked up the microphone. "Ladies and gentlemen, let's hear it for Mr. and Mrs. Chris McAllister," he announced in a booming baritone, and the audience happily complied. Their boisterous applause and shouts of approval could probably be heard in Phoenix, Max thought wryly. Then he noticed Logan's expression. It hadn't changed at all. As far as Logan was concerned, he and Eden might have been all alone in the world.

I wonder if I look like that when I'm with Cretia? he asked himself. The thought made him go in search of her. He reached the cake table just as the DJ said, "Let's join them, folks. Come on. Let's dance!"

"Dance?" he asked, holding out his hand to her.

"Can't," she said, her expression forlorn. "I still need to cut up wedding cake."

Lydia wasn't accepting that. "There's no line left, Mom," she said. "Nobody's waiting, and Marcie and I can handle anybody who still wants a piece later, or comes back for seconds."

"Sure we can," Marcie said. Max tossed her a grateful look. "You go ahead and dance with Daddy."

"Come on," he urged Cretia. She seemed reluctant, but wasn't too hard to persuade. As he drew her onto the dance floor, he called over his shoulder, "Save some of that wedding cake for me!"

"Will do, Dad," Marcie answered.

"They're good girls," Max observed as he took heaven in his arms.

"Yes, they are." Cretia melted against him.

"You're melting," he observed. "You and that cake of yours."

She smiled. "For a while there, I thought it wasn't going to make it."

"You did just great," he said, his voice filled with pride. "You pulled that off like a trooper, and there wasn't a soul out here who had any idea what we'd gone through by the time the cake came out. It looked just splendid, a real triumph."

"I have you to thank for that."

Her voice was low and sweet. It sounded as good as she smelled. She smelled as good as she looked. Her kiss tasted . . . He wondered how she tasted now, with bits of sweet icing on her tongue. The effect on Max was immediate and startling. No wonder he thought instantly of fireworks. "I hear there's a good fireworks show in Holbrook tonight," he said evenly, proud of the calm in his voice. "Would you and the kids like to go with me?"

Cretia lifted her head off his shoulder so she could look at him. "Yes," she said. "Yes, I would. And Max?"

"Hmm?"

"Thanks for asking me first."

"First?"

"Yeah. As opposed to getting the kids on your side, then asking me after everyone else is already lined up."

"Oh." He paused, drawing her a little closer. "I didn't realize it bothered you so much when I did that. I'll try to be careful in the future."

The grateful smile she beamed at him could have warmed him all winter. "Thanks, Max."

"Don't mention it."

"I'm already looking forward to it."

His brow furrowed. "To what?" *Is it possible she knows all the things I've been thinking? Heavens! I hope not!*

"To the fireworks," she said, sensibly. "Had you forgotten already?"

"No, I just . . . Never mind." He stopped trying to make conversation after that, content simply to hold her, swaying to the music. *I'll bet I look a lot like Logan*, he thought, smiling down at her. *And why shouldn't I?*

Good question, he responded, chatting again with his little voice. *Why shouldn't I, indeed?* As he steered her into the middle of the dance area, and into a steadily thickening crowd of dancers, he pondered that question, already sure of the answer. If Logan looked that way because he was smitten, then it made sense that he too should look just like that. After all, Cretia made him feel powerful, capable, cared for, cherished, and more than just a little bit in love.

Chapter Seven

The first rocket burst red and gold in the night sky and the crowd ahhed appreciatively. Some spectators cheered and others honked their car horns to encourage the show to go forward.

"Are the fireworks finally starting?" Danny asked. He sat up, rubbing sleep from his eyes.

"Looks like it," Cretia answered, and tucked a light blanket around her son's shoulders as they all sat cuddled together in the back of Chris's truck.

Chris, who had taken his town car on his honeymoon, had left his pickup truck for Max, just for this purpose. "The fireworks show in Holbrook is one of the best small-town shows you'll ever see," he had told Max sometime earlier, "but you need a pickup truck to see it properly." He had described to Max how to park his truck with the rear facing the bluff where the rockets were fired, and how to take sleeping bags and lots of blankets to make a comfortable nest for everyone to sit in while they watched the show. Max had already been in Rainbow Rock long enough to understand how the high desert could be cooking temperature at midday and bone-chilling cold by the time it got dark, so he hadn't argued with Chris about the blankets, but had come well prepared for the crisp evening air.

It's been a beautiful day, Cretia reflected as she snuggled against the man who sat at her other side, drawing her son with her. *It's been a beautiful, memorable day, and I have Max Carmody to thank for it.*

He had certainly saved her this morning when he had come through with his "giant toothpicks" that had held the wedding cake together. The cake had turned out beautifully—one of her best—and she had taken plenty of pictures with her own camera, not to mention all the pictures the various McAllisters had taken, before they wheeled it into the outside heat. After that, Chris and Sarah had quickly cut the cake and served pieces to each other, so it hadn't taken long at all before the top layer had been saved for the future and the rest was in the process of being cut and eaten. All of it had happened fast enough to keep the frosting from puddling at the base. As a result, the cake she had worked so hard to create—and she couldn't forget how Max had helped her with that part, either—had been a triumph, rather than a tragedy, and had further enhanced her reputation in the community.

Cretia couldn't forget how she had depended on that reputation and the word-of-mouth business it had brought her many times in the past when doing specialty cakes for people throughout Navajo County had been the only way she could pull together extra cash for birthdays or Christmas or other family occasions, or even to get the kids' new school clothes in the fall.

Another rocket went up and Cretia allowed herself to relax and enjoy the show, letting go of every cautious or unhappy thought. *Maybe I won't need to do cakes in the future*, she thought happily as she responded to a comment Max had made about the fireworks. Now that she was working as a producer full-time, her salary was finally covering all the necessities without stretching, and even allowing room for some extras. *In another month, I'll be able to buy Max's car if I want to*, she calculated, wondering then whether she'd feel comfortable about buying that car from Max, or whether she should start looking for another car of her own. As much as she enjoyed Max's gold sedan, she feared it would be giving up a little of her hard-won independence if she accepted his choice, rather than making a choice of her own.

"Ooh, look, Mom!" Lydia called as the next rocket exploded. The bits of brilliant flame formed a happy face in the sky.

"Mom, can I have another cookie?" Danny asked.

"Sure, honey. Help yourself," Cretia said, pulling the cookie bag closer to her son.

Max had even come through with the tailgate picnic they had enjoyed while waiting for the fireworks this evening. He had gone to some trouble to come up with roasted chicken, sliced vegetables and pieces of fruit, crackers, chips and dip. Cretia had brought some homemade oatmeal-raisin cookies she had frozen a couple of weeks earlier, and a large chunk of leftover wedding cake to create their dessert. Max had brought along a cooler full of soda cans and fruit juices in single servings. It seemed he'd thought of everything.

He had even helped Danny build the kite he had planned for this afternoon, though they'd had to strip a couple of twigs from her flowering plum tree to replace the dowelings that had saved her cake. Danny hadn't minded. He'd spent so many hours chasing after that kite that he'd exhausted himself, falling asleep in the warm nest in the back of Chris's truck as soon as their dinner was over, dozing to the strains of "Eine Kleine Nachtmusik," played on Max's boom box.

"You've been a real knight in shining armor today,"

Cretia murmured, snuggling closer to Max as the kids oohed and ahhed at the next volley of rockets. "Thanks, Max, for everything."

"No problem," he answered, putting his arm around her and gathering her closer, but she saw the pride in his response. He had enjoyed being there for her. That was nice in itself. She couldn't remember the last time that "being there" for Cretia had been a priority for anyone.

It's even a perfect evening, thanks to Max, Cretia thought, watching as the local fire department set off the first of several ground-based displays that used the backdrop of the bluffs to advantage. This display was a waterfall, its "falls" made of white fire rather than water, pouring from a high point on the bluff and splashing down its sides. The crowd applauded and cheered, as did their little group in the back of the pickup.

Our little family group, Cretia thought, allowing herself the fantasy for the moment. They'd had such a delightful day together, first at the wedding and reception, even dancing for a while, later helping with cleanup and enjoying one another's company, then with the kite and finally with the picnic and fireworks. The girls had become a matched set, inseparable and apparently enjoying every minute of the time they spent together. Even little Danny apparently had great fun, only once stopping to complain that now *both* Lydia and Marcie were breaking the One-Mommy-Per-Person Rule. Cretia's fantasy of a perfect day with a perfect family was playing out nicely.

And now we're having a perfect Fourth of July evening. The night had chosen to cooperate, dropping temperatures into the middle 60s to give them enough cool for cuddling, but keeping the breeze down so the cool of evening was pleasant rather than brisk. Even the moon was putting off her appearance until later, allowing a star-spangled black sky for the county's pyrotechnics.

"Oh, look!" Marcie shouted as another volley burst into the sky, synchronized so one burst of glory broke just as the one before it glimmered out.

"Beautiful," Max agreed, though she noticed he looked at her as he said it.

There was another ground display then, a yards-long American flag painted in brilliant red, white, and blue flame, shimmering along the lower ridge of the bluff above them. The crowd cheered and honked their horns in appreciation, continuing the applause for more than half a minute while the flag shimmered and flamed before them.

"It's beautiful," Lydia said, her tone reverential.

"Yes, isn't it?" Cretia agreed. *This whole day has been beautiful. Thank you, Max. Thank you so much.* She looked up at him then, smiling her gratitude, and caught him watching her again, his eyes full of tenderness. Cretia felt her heart swell. Having Max care about her was the greatest blessing she'd known in years. *Worth having,* she thought, *even if only for a little while.* She knew that Max was helping her heal her heart, teaching her to trust again, maybe in time, even to love again. She could never thank him enough for that, not even when he went away, leaving her alone.

"Oh, another one! Look!" Danny pointed, and Cretia dutifully appreciated the multiple rockets that filled the sky to the right of the bluff, taking the attention away from the flag display, which had almost burned out now. For a few minutes, the show continued, and Cretia relaxed, content just to be in the moment, with these great kids, and this good man.

"They're lighting another ground display," Lydia said a few minutes later.

"I see," Cretia answered, noting where the flashlights played on the rocks above them, showing where the firefighters were preparing another spectacle.

"I wonder what this one will be," Max said as the flames began to burn. "It sure seems to have a lot of color in it."

"Purple, red, blue . . ." Marcie counted off as the colors lighted, then spread.

"I know what it is!" Danny said. "It's a—"

"A rainbow!" Lydia, Marcie, and Danny all finished his sentence in unison.

"Daddy, it's a rainbow!" Marcie called, her voice filled with wonder. "It's a rainbow shining in the night sky, just like you said!"

"It's a night rainbow, Mom!" Lydia spoke almost before Marcie had finished.

"You know what this means, don't you?" Marcie said to Lydia.

Cretia looked up at Max, who looked helplessly at her, just as Lydia and Marcie both spoke, the two of them answering Marcie's question: "We're getting married!"

"Now wait a minute," Max said. Cretia thought he might have been responding to the silent request he had just spotted in her eyes.

"But that's what you said, Daddy." Marcie was making it clear just how she felt about the idea.

"It was what you said, too, Mom," Lydia reminded.

"I said I'd be *thinking* about it," Max emphasized.

"Don't push, Lydia," Cretia warned, unwilling to trust her voice with anything more than that. She was feeling too choked up, too sentimental, too frightened. Who had imagined that fate would send them a night rainbow just when she needed one? *And who can guess what Max will say about it?*

The rainbow was burning out as the crowd's attention turned to the next burst of fireworks. The kids reluctantly turned their attention as well. Max turned to Cretia and she felt a momentary anxiety about what he might say. "I never thought I'd see the day," he whispered quietly.

"I know what you mean," she answered, glad his comment had been so neutral, and so calmly delivered. "I never thought I'd see it, either. I never would have guessed there really was such a thing as a night rainbow."

"I don't mean that," Max said, dropping his voice so his words, whispered against her ear, were for Cretia alone to hear. "I mean, I never thought I'd see the day when my daughter would try to talk me into a second marriage."

"Oh, that," Cretia answered, nearly breathless at what might come next. *How many ways can a man find to tell you he doesn't want you?* she asked herself, trying to prepare for whichever way Max might pick.

"What's even more amazing to me," he said, with the air of a man who was choosing each word, "is I find I'm actually thinking about it."

Cretia raised her eyebrows, amazed at the note of hope that had crept into her voice. "You are?"

He kissed her hair, then her ear. "I am," he whispered, "and the idea scares me less every day."

"Oh," Cretia said, and then stopped talking as Max's mouth came down upon hers, stopping all speech, even stopping her thoughts.

In the dim distance, she heard her son's voice. "They're kissing again," Danny grumbled.

"Shh, Danny," Lydia said. "Shut up and watch the fireworks."

"I am," Danny answered. "I am."

Max set the ratchet down on the workbench and wiped his brow. *How can I be sure?* he asked himself, slugging down the rest of the bottled water he had brought into D. J.'s this morning. *How can you ever be sure?*

It had been five days since the Fourth of July fireworks—all of them—and he and Cretia had spent as much time as possible together, including a fine weekend when her kids were away with their dad and he had found excuses to leave Marcie "helping Meg with the baby." They had picnicked at Cholla Lake, had eaten out at the local Thai restaurant, and had even baked another cake together, this one a relatively simple chocolate fudge creation special-ordered for the fiftieth birthday of a woman Cretia knew from church. They'd played a game of Rook with Lydia and Marcie. They had listened to all their favorite Mozart music during a long session in Cretia's living room, talking about their favorite passages and what they liked best about each. They had even spent one quiet evening watching an old romantic movie alone together, cuddled in each other's arms. What they hadn't done was talk about marriage, not so much as a mention of the M word.

That hadn't kept their kids from mentioning it, as frequently as possible and especially in their presence. Even the guy at the counter of the wrecking yard in Winslow, where he and Danny had gone to buy alternators, had gotten an earful about how "Max and Mom" were thinking about getting married. He had practically had to pick the kid up under one arm and haul him out of there to keep him from making a public announcement.

He smiled now, just thinking of that day with Danny. *Okay, so maybe I'm not sure, but it's nice to know the kids wouldn't object.* Max grimaced at himself. *Okay, okay, it's more than just not objecting. They want us to be together, all five of us. They want the power and security of family.*

Then, *Well, why not? Don't I want that, too? Haven't I always? I just don't know whether I have that in me. I certainly didn't give my best to Joanna, and Marcie was half-grown before she really knew she had a dad.*

He felt the familiar thrum of guilt pulse through him, the guilt he always felt whenever he thought of Marcie and the way he had ignored most of her childhood. Then, with a touch of surprise, he realized the guilt was lessening. These past weeks in Rainbow Rock had done much to diminish his remorse over Marcie, and a great deal to bring him closer to her.

I know her now, Max thought as he picked up the ratchet and gave it another hard turn. *Before, she was just another kid. The only difference was she was the one I was responsible for. Now . . . now she's a person to me.* He thought of the sly little grin she always managed to flash at him when they were partnering at Rook and she had a good bidding hand. He knew that look now, just as he knew that she "loved" anything purple, or in any of the fifty shades of lavender, lilac, and whatever that all looked purple to him, but "loathed" anything pink. He knew the types of popular music she preferred, and that she was deliberately trying to cultivate an interest in Mozart, just to please him. He knew she had a pleasant singing voice, that she felt awkward at school dances, and that she liked Mexican food, but thought Chinese mustard was "just too hot." He even knew the names of her favorite teen heartthrobs, especially the ones she and Lydia liked in common. *I know her*, he thought again, a little awed by the discovery, *and I like what I know.*

He raised an eyebrow. *I may have to thank my interfering sister for forcing the issue*, he thought. A new discovery washed over him as he realized he was happily thinking of Meg as his sister—his real sister—and not as the pushy, distant half relative he barely knew. *I've gained a lot of family these past weeks*, he thought, surprised at how much gratitude he felt.

But am I ready to take on a ready-made family of my own? A wife? Three kids? And would there be three? What would Joanna say if I wanted to keep Marcella with me, with us? I'd have to go house-shopping, too. My little condo in Santa Ana wouldn't hold us all. And I'd have to work it out for the kids to transfer schools. . . .

The idea was becoming overwhelming, so full of big decisions, frightening ones. *And I don't want to mess them up this time.* Max dropped the ratchet with a sigh. *So how can I be sure I'm doing the right thing?* He was wise enough to realize that people he cared deeply for would be hurt if he broke things off now. *But will I hurt them more if I try and fail?* he wondered. *Or is that just an excuse to keep me from making the effort?*

Then, disgusted with himself, he put the ratchet back on D. J.'s rack and started cleaning up around him. He still had a lot to do to get ready before he brought over the full engine he'd bought at the auto yard that day with Danny. Replacing the whole engine was the only way he could think of to rebuild Cretia's old clunker. Still . . . *Too much heavy thinking for a hot afternoon,* he told himself. *I need a cool shower, a colder drink, and a visit with Cretia. Maybe I'll clean up first, then drop in on her at the office.* It amazed him how quickly that idea lifted his spirits.

"Color balance is okay. Looks like we're ready." Cretia set down her clipboard and checklists. "Camera A?" She turned to Kurt.

"A's rolling."

"Thank you. Camera B?" This time she looked in the opposite direction, toward Kurt's friend, Stan, recruited for this shoot.

"B's rolling," Stan answered.

"Sound cheek." Self-nominated as the sound engineer for today's shoot, she put on the earphones and checked her monitor. "Sound level's good," she said. "Okay, Jim. Whenever you're ready." She gave him the "go" sign and listened carefully as he did his standard intro.

It had taken a lot of setting up to get them ready for this interview of the woman Jim called his "little grandmother" in English or *'Ama-sani* in her own tongue. Clara Begay had become steadily more sought after and increasingly re-clusive since her big sale at Sotheby's a couple of years back. As popular as handmade rugs had become, few weav-ers could command a cool half-million for their work. Had they not had Jim to give them entrée . . . Well, Cretia was just glad they had. It was a break for her, too. She was directing this interview, as well as producing it.

What was that? She looked quickly at the monitor, which was moving along just fine, measuring the highs and lows of Jim's opening speech. *There it is again, a sort of scratching sound.* This time she was looking at the monitor when she heard it; the monitor heard it, too.

"Cut, cut," she cried, waving her hands and bringing the scene to a halt.

"What's up?" Kurt asked, obviously annoyed.

"A scratching sound. It was small, but I heard it. Twice."

Kurt curled his lip in frustration. "Jim probably just has his mike rubbing against his collar."

"No. I checked that before we started. It's something else, like a mechanical problem."

"You checked out the sound system before we left the studio," Kurt groused, his voice volume rising. Stan cleared his throat uncomfortably.

"Yes, I did," Cretia answered, "and everything checked out then."

"Why don't I just adjust my microphone?" Jim asked helpfully, and began fumbling with the clip.

"Here, let me," Cretia said, helping him get the mike near his face, but free enough so it wouldn't rub on his collar or hair. "There, that should do it." She went back to her place. "Okay. Rolling?"

"Rolling," Kurt answered.

"Rolling," echoed Stan.

"On five," she cued. "Four, three . . ." She gave Jim

the "go" sign and he started the intro again. He'd almost finished it before the scratch came again, louder this time. Cretia looked quickly at the monitor, then at Jim's mike, which was clearly riding free. Just as she looked back at the monitor, the sound came again, then again. It happened every time Kurt moved his camera cable, and it was louder every time it happened.

"Cut!" she called again.

"What is it this time?" Kurt bellowed.

"I think we've got a cable problem, Kurt," Cretia answered levelly. "Every time you move that camera enough to make the cable move, the scratch is clear, and it's getting louder all the time."

"You're not just imagining this?" Kurt was clearly unhappy.

The thought occurred to Cretia that as the owner of the company she worked for, Kurt was her boss. Still, when they were on the shoot, she was quality control. She had to report what she heard. "No, Kurt. I'm not making this up," she answered evenly. "We've got a problem, and I think it's in your camera cable."

"That's ridiculous!" Kurt said. "The camera's in top shape, and it's never given us trouble before."

"That's no guarantee it can't give us trouble now," she answered, "and trouble is just what it's giving us. Do you have a backup cable for that camera?"

"Sure, back in the studio."

"Nothing here?"

"Of course not! It's not like I bring the whole setup with me when we go on location."

"Then we'll have to shoot the scene twice from two different angles. We'll use Stan's camera." She turned to speak to Stan.

"No way." Kurt got in front of her. "Let's work out the sound problem or ignore it and move on. We set up this two-camera shoot for a reason and it's costing us money.''

"It would cost us more to have to redo it, Kurt." Cretia could feel her pulse picking up. Arguing with the boss wasn't smart, but what could she do?

"Then we'll edit out the scratch in post. Come on, let's roll.''

Cretia took a deep breath. "No, Kurt. Postproduction editing can fix lots of things, but this sound is loud and getting louder, and it's erratic. I don't think you can fix it in post. We need to shoot the interview with one camera, or not shoot it at all. Not today, anyway.''

"Cretia . . ." Kurt's voice was threatening.

"Okay, Kurt. Let's call it the way it is. You're the owner, the boss. Fire me if you want, but you made me the director today, and on my own authority I'm telling you that we can't work with that camera today, not unless we can repair or replace the cable.''

For a moment they stood toe-to-toe while Jim and Stan looked on nervously and Clara Begay, who understood little English, watched with an interested, though bewildered, expression. Finally Kurt stepped back.

"Okay, Cretia. You're the director. We'll play it your way. But I want to see what Meg has to say about this when we get back to the studio.''

"Fine with me," Cretia answered, and turned her back on him. "Stan, you're rolling.''

"Rolling,'' he said, as Cretia turned off Camera A.

"Then we're on," Cretia said, ignoring the fact that Kurt was storming off across the hills. "On five, four, three . . .'' She signaled Jim and the taping began.

"I agree,'' Meg was saying. "That's exactly how I would have handled it myself.''

Cretia couldn't help grinning, warmed through by Meg's

approval. She was rapidly learning to trust her instincts in the situations and problems that arose as they were taping, but it helped when her more-experienced boss confirmed her choices. "Good, I'm glad you approve," she answered. "I figure we'll get the camera into the shop as quickly as possible so we don't have to handle things the same way in New Mexico next weekend."

"That should work just fine," Meg answered.

"That is, if Kurt's still speaking to me, or willing to work with me. He sulked all the way home."

"Kurt's just fine." Kurt himself walked out of the back room. "I've been listening to the tapes of the first couple of attempts and you were right. It was the cable and we wouldn't have been able to fix it in post. I'm glad we had you there to catch that, Cretia, and I apologize."

Cretia finally relaxed. "No problem," she answered, smiling her relief.

"Nah, it *is* a problem," Kurt said. It was clear he had embarrassed himself. "I don't like to behave like a jerk. It just seems to come naturally whenever somebody questions my work."

"Kurt, you know I wasn't questioning—"

"I know. At least, I know it now. Sorry. Knee-jerk reaction, I guess."

Cretia offered her hand. "Everything's fine, then?"

He solemnly shook it. "Better than fine. We owe you. You're doing great work for us." He gave her a snappy military salute, then winked as he walked out.

"Wow," she said, raising her brows at Meg just as the bell on the office front door jingled.

Cretia looked up just in time to see Max enter, his face alive with anticipation. As always, it warmed her to realize this handsome, powerful, very attractive man was looking so eagerly for her. She stood. "Hi, Max. To what do we owe this honor?"

His grin pleased her. "I thought I'd drop in to see if you have plans for lunch. Maybe if you don't, I can talk you into sharing a plate of Navajo tacos with me down at the Kachina."

"Navajo tacos sound great." She looked toward Meg. "That okay with you, boss? Will you be around to handle things here for a while?"

Meg was wearing a grin that would have honored the Cheshire Cat. "You two just go ahead and enjoy lunch," she said smugly. "I'll handle whatever comes up here. But you know," Meg added as Cretia sorted her paperwork, "between your production schedule and your social calendar, I think we may have to start looking for a new receptionist."

"That sounds like a good idea," Cretia said, pleased by all the undertones she had heard in Meg's little speech. The day was coming when someone else would take over all the small clerical errands she still came in to do when they weren't taping. Soon she would have completely outgrown the job that had almost overwhelmed her when she'd started here a couple of years ago. She felt the growth she had experienced since then, and she thrilled at it. There had been so many years when she hadn't felt capable of handling an average day. Now she was handling so much more than she had ever thought possible, and doing it well. She felt strong, capable, powerful. It was a heady sensation.

They left the office, Max offering his arm and Cretia taking it as they strolled along the sidewalk toward the Kachina Café. Trying to keep her voice calm, Cretia asked, "Did you just miss me? Or did you have something special in mind?"

"I think I want to talk about us," Max said, his voice tentative.

Cretia felt the rush of emotions. She wasn't sure whether eagerness or dread prevailed, but she knew there was some hope and terror mixed in as well. "Maybe it's time we did," she said, stopping and looking Max squarely in the eye. "What about us?"

"Ever since the night rainbow . . ." Max paused. They'd reached the door of the Kachina. "Shall we go in and order first?"

"I'm not very hungry," Cretia answered evenly. Only half an hour ago she'd been telling Meg that if she didn't find something to eat soon, she was going to start chewing on her paperweight. *Funny how circumstances can change your priorities*, she thought as she added, "I could eat, though, if you're hungry."

"Maybe we could just talk for a while first?" Max looked as nervous as she felt.

"Okay," she said. "There's a bench in front of the courthouse."

He nodded and they started in that direction. "What do you think of the idea?" he asked, "Strictly hypothetically, of course. Do you think we can talk about . . . ? Could we consider . . . ?"

His discomfort tickled Cretia's funny bone and she giggled. Then, embarrassed at herself, she said, "I'm sorry, Max. It does seem to be difficult for both of us, doesn't it?"

"It shouldn't be," he said. "People get married all the time."

She took a deep breath. "Is that what we're talking about, Max? Getting married?"

"I just thought I'd ask what you think of the idea. It would involve a lot of changes. . . ."

"Yes, it would." Cretia waited.

They had reached the courthouse and Max gestured toward the bench. Cretia sat and he took the space beside her, then took her hands into his. "I guess I just want to know how you feel about me, about us. Do you think we could make it work? I mean . . .'' He paused, swallowing hard. Cretia sympathized. ''Would you be willing to take a chance on me, Cretia? You know I wasn't much of a husband before, or much of a father.''

Cretia met his eyes clearly. ''Are you asking me if I'm in love with you, Max?''

He chuckled, a nervous sound, but sobered quickly. ''I suppose I am, but it's more than that, Cretia. We aren't young, starry-eyed kids with no responsibilities to anyone but each other. We've both made mistakes. We have children, separate lives. . . . I guess I'm just wondering if, as a practical matter, you think we could make it work.''

''Practical matters, is it?'' She tried to keep the disappointment from her voice. ''I must say, Max. You could quite sweep me off my feet with a proposal like that.''

This time Max's chuckle was more genuine. ''I do sound like a heel, don't I?''

''A heel, Max?'' She smiled. ''A supercilious jerk, maybe. An unromantic pain-in-the—''

''Cretia!'' Max laughed, surprised at both of them. ''You're right. I'm botching this rather badly.''

She smiled, relenting a little. ''I didn't cut you much slack, did I?''

''Why should you?'' he said, turning the tables on himself. ''I should have gotten on my knees and sworn my undying love, promised you roses and diamonds as I threw myself at your feet. I guess I'm just afraid that none of that means much when the problems begin. I guess I was hoping we could have a discussion about how we'd live, how we'd solve the problems as they arise. I guess I was—''

''Stop, Max.'' She gentled her speech. ''I don't want to hear about the problems. Not now. Can we postpone this whole discussion for later? Another time?''

''Okay,'' he said. ''Will you just tell me you're thinking about it, too?''

"Every day," she promised. "Every day."

They ended their discussion with a gentle kiss.

It was Friday, July 11. Two days had passed since the attempted discussion on the courthouse bench, and Max was going home—only, oddly, it felt more like leaving home, now that he stood on the blacktop at the Holbrook Municipal Airport, preparing to board a small plane that would carry him to Sky Harbor in Phoenix, then a larger one to take him to LAX.

"Does it feel funny, leaving like this?" he asked Marcie, who stood at his side as the little plane rolled into boarding position.

"Yeah. Really funny," his daughter answered. "Like I'm taking a trip, not like going home at all."

"I know what you mean," Max said, impressed by Marcie's insight.

The idea had come up quickly. He had walked Cretia back to the office after their chat at the courthouse and had found Meg talking with Kurt about plans to shoot in New Mexico the next week. A new opportunity had come up and Meg thought Cretia and Kurt should arrange to take a few days, covering everything they could get while they were there. She explained it all to Cretia while Max listened.

"So I guess I'd better pack some bags and see what I can arrange for the kids," Cretia had said as she finished.

Immediately, Max saw red. Or was it green? "You and Kurt, traveling together? Overnight? What does his wife think of this idea?"

"Alexa?" Cretia had answered, eyes wide. "She's going with us, of course."

"Oh. Of course." Cursing himself for a fool, Max had relented, and had listened more attentively as the rest of the plans were described. "So what can I do to help while you're gone?" he asked after a time.

"I'm not sure," Cretia had said. "Let me make a few phone calls." Minutes later she reported, "Danny says since this is his make-up weekend with the kids, anyway, he will be happy to keep them until we're back on Wednesday, maybe Thursday."

"So you're set then," Meg contributed. "All you need to do is get your things together."

"Looks like. Do you think maybe Kurt and Alexa would be willing to leave Friday morning instead of waiting? We could try to catch that woman in Gallup on our way over to Window Rock."

"That might work. Let me see."

Within minutes the trip was planned and Cretia was getting ready to leave at dawn on Friday. Feeling at loose ends as he left the office, Max had found a pay phone and used his calling card to reach his production manager at the auto parts factory. "Long time, no hear," Nate had said. "I thought you were losing interest in what goes on around here."

"Not losing interest. Just learning that you handle it fine without me," Max lied smoothly, amazed to realize that he *had* lost interest, at least to the degree that the auto parts factory was no longer the single consuming passion of his life. "So did you get the plans I faxed you for a new replacement alternator?"

"Yeah, they look great. I've had several of the guys here look them over and they grasped your concept immediately. They also think a working prototype should be fairly easy to come up with. John Riley says—" Nate had gone on for some time, reporting on the positive opinions everyone seemed to share about Max's latest idea.

"By the way, Max," he said as he finished, "we've just about completed alpha testing on the new water pump, and we're getting ready to install the working models in several staff cars here to do a basic beta test. I'd sure like you to see how the prototype is working.''

"That sounds like an idea," Max had responded, and by the end of the afternoon, he too had been packing his bags, getting ready for a few days away. Cretia had thought it a great solution, something to keep Max occupied and interested while she was away working hard, and when Marcie had reported that her mother had talked about missing her during their latest telephone visit, Max's trip had quickly been planned for two. Now he and Marcie boarded the light plane together, headed back to Orange County, but unsure whether they were going home or leaving it. If home was where the heart was, Max had a hunch he was leaving it behind.

The next Wednesday afternoon, as he and Marcie stood in line at LAX, awaiting the boarding call for their return flight, Max was sure he had been right. Everything had changed in the weeks that he had been away, everything. His little condo had been pleasant, efficient—and sterile, not a thing in it to speak of "home." The factory had been great, better than ever in fact. Nate had proudly shown him productivity schedules that made him feel he should have left town years ago. June had been their very best summer month on record, and July was already poised to become their best month ever. Sales were up; new contracts were increasing. In fact, if he hadn't known better, he'd have sworn his business was better off without him.

That had given him some cause for pause, and he had asked Nate about it on Wednesday morning, just a few hours before they left. "Tell me honestly, Nate," he'd begun as they did a final walk-through of the production floor, "and don't worry about sparing the boss's feelings."

"Okay, boss. What is it?"

"How come you're getting so much better production with me away?"

"My honest opinion?" Nate had asked carefully, and Max had nodded, afraid he wasn't going to like this at all.

"You're a brilliant engineer, Max, and an okay manager, but just okay. You have your own set of specialty skills that nobody here can equal. In all the years that Carmody Auto Parts has been in business, nobody has innovated a new part that actually worked in testing, but in the course of the last few weeks, you've come up with a great one, possibly two. Your skills in engineering and innovation are legendary, but your skill as a manager sometimes leaves something to be desired."

"That's why I hired you, isn't it?" Max could hear the petulance in his voice, but couldn't seem to keep it from coming through.

"That's right, Max. You hired me to do it, but until you went away, you never *let* me do it, not really. Your tendency is to micro-manage everything, rather than letting your people do the work you hired them to do. Then, because you spend so much of your time handling all the little details that the rest of us could be managing if you'd let us, you don't have the time for innovation and invention that could really move Carmody Auto forward in the future. It's not your best use of either your own time and skills, or ours."

Max bit his lip. "Whew! I asked for that one, didn't I?"

"I'm not trying to hurt your feelings, Max, but how long has it been since you've come up with a new replacement part? Until this summer, I mean?"

"Never," Max admitted reluctantly. "Not since the first day we geared up for production."

"Exactly. But here you are with a few weeks away from the day-to-day management of the place and you've come up with a great new water pump, and an alternator that looks like it's going to be a genuine winner. I wouldn't be surprised if you've got a great deal more innovation in you, too, just waiting to come out, but only so long as you stay away from the plant and let us handle things here.''

''Wow,'' Max had said quietly. ''You're really giving me something to chew on here, Nate.''

''It's your company, of course,'' Nate went on, ''and I'm not about to tell you what to do with it, but if I were you . . .''

''Yeah, Nate. Go on.''

''I'd think about staying away. Permanently. Set up a machine shop off premises, maybe at or near your home, and focus on creating new products. Let those of us who know the day-to-day stuff take over here. Come in now and then for policy-setting and problem-solving, or just for regular updates with the staff. Other than that, do your own thing and let us do ours.''

''I'll think about that,'' Max had said as he prepared to leave. ''I'll think about doing just that.'' And he had thought about it, all afternoon. His factory was better off without him. Who would have thought it? It wasn't exactly flattering, but it was thought-provoking. Maybe Nate had a point about using his own best talents and letting others use theirs.

''You okay, Daddy?'' Marcie had asked, aware of her father's absorption.

''Yes, honey.'' He made the effort to turn his attention. ''How was your visit home with your mom?''

''It was okay.'' Marcie didn't meet his eyes, then she did. ''But, Daddy? I'm eager to go home again, back to Rainbow Rock, I mean.''

''I know what you mean,'' he said as they heard the first boarding call. ''I know exactly what you mean.''

When he finally got off the small plane onto the tarmac in Holbrook at some late, dark hour and saw Cretia eagerly waiting to greet him, he knew how right they were.

Chapter Eight

He first got the idea while watching Meg and Jim prepare for a long weekend in the White Mountains with Kurt and Alexa. It grew on him as he watched them load their gear into the back of Kurt's pickup. By the time he drove to Cretia's house, he was sure it was the perfect thing. Convincing her was another story, as he learned that Friday evening.

"You want us to do *what?*" She looked as if he'd suggested grub-eating or grave-robbing, not a simple camping trip.

"Camping, Cretia. It's a common recreation. Lots of people do it."

"Not *my* people." She slammed the spatula she'd been holding into the sink.

"Come on, honey," he cajoled her. "What's the problem? Meg and Jim own lots of great equipment—tents, sleeping bags, a propane stove and lantern—the works! And they've promised to let us borrow anything we need. It'll be easy, and it might be lots of fun."

"Sleeping on the ground is *not* my idea of fun."

"Would air mattresses help? They have those, too."

142

"Air mattresses, huh?" At least she wasn't slamming things around anymore.

"Sure. Nice ones. And lots of other nifty gadgets." He stepped close behind her and ran his hands along her arms. "I know you've got vacation time coming. I asked your boss. And this would be a great way for all of us to get away together, all properly chaperoned—one tent for the Sherwoods and one for the Carmodys."

"Won't the girls want to be together?"

"Okay. One for the women and one for the men. I'll enjoy roughin' it with Danny."

"Roughin' it, huh? I thought you were trying to talk me *into* this."

"Good point. How about I promise to do all, or at least most, of the cooking. You won't have to lift a finger except to have a good time."

"I'm going to eat your cooking and still have a good time?" She flashed him a doubtful look.

He grabbed his chest. "Ouch. That one hurt. And here I am trying to be a good guy."

"A veritable hero." She paused, chewing her lip. "Let's say I agree to this foolishness. Where would you want to go?"

"Marcie has never seen the Grand Canyon," Max said. "It's under a hundred miles from here, so we could make it in an easy drive and have plenty of time to set up. I figure if we planned four or five days, that would give us lots of time to see everything there is to see—from the South Rim, anyway—and maybe even get in some hiking."

"Hiking? In the Canyon?"

"Only if we decide we want to."

"And if we were really miserable? What then?"

"If you decided you were really miserable . . ." He took a deep breath, trying to gauge what she might accept. "If you were really unhappy after the first night, I'd check everybody into the hotel. My treat.''

Her answer was sharp. "Really, Max. You have to stop throwing your money at me.''

"Okay. If you were miserable and you didn't want to check into the hotel, we could come home the next day.''

She sighed. "And I'd be the bad guy again.''

"If that's your concern, I promise I'd tell the kids it was my idea.'' He stepped closer, stroking her back. "Come on, Cretia. Give it a try. It would give us a chance to spend some time together without distractions. We could all get to know one another better, see if we get on one another's nerves in close quarters, and sometimes, you and I could send the kids off to look at something by themselves while we took long walks alone. It would give us time to talk about . . . well, about us.''

She paused. He could tell she was considering the idea. "When would you want to go?''

"Let's get out the calendar,'' he said. A few minutes later they had decided on a week from the next Monday, leaving early and coming back before dusk the following Friday, the first day of August. "Just wait and see. You're gonna love this,'' Max promised as he headed for his car, eager to begin making plans.

"Assuming you can get reservations,'' she said. He thought she looked rather too hopeful about the possibility that he couldn't.

"Reservations will be no problem,'' he assured.

He found it was more difficult than he'd thought, but with patience and repeated phone calls, he was able to reserve a space within the national park, not far from the hotel and gift shop on the Canyon's south rim. Congratulating himself, he called Cretia, who accepted the news the way a prisoner might have accepted a long sentence.

"Really, babe," he assured her. "It's going to be good. I promise."

"You know," she said, "I think maybe it could be. I never went camping much as a kid, but I remember it as a really awful experience, with inadequate sleeping bags on the hard ground and an old canvas tent that leaked in the rain. . . . Dad was trying to cook over an open campfire—"

"In the rain?" Max asked, incredulous. "No wonder you had such an awful experience."

"Yup. Later, when the kids were little, Danny insisted we should take them camping. We tried it a couple of times, and I remember we had some mattress pads and the tent was dry, but Danny always took a cooler full of beer and that led to—"

"Don't tell me," Max growled, thinking again that if he ever got his hands on Danny Sherwood, he might forget he'd once promised himself never to harm another human being. "I get the picture. It's not surprising that, with memories like those, you might not be very eager to try it again."

"No." He could hear water running and he realized she was working at the sink as they talked. "That's what I've been thinking since you left here a while ago. Maybe the only thing I have against camping is the poor quality of a few past experiences. Maybe I really ought to give it another shot."

"I think you'll enjoy it," he said gently. "I really do. I wouldn't have suggested it otherwise."

"I believe you," she said, "about your good intentions, anyway. As for the rest . . . Well, we can't really know until we give it a try, can we?"

"Exactly," he said, "and we'll do a lot of careful planning during this coming week, making sure we're prepared for every contingency. So do you want to tell the kids, or should I?"

"Why don't you and Marcie come over tomorrow for breakfast? We'll poll the constituents then."

"Sounds good. What can I bring?"

"I'll make waffles," she answered, and he thought her voice sounded firmer. "Maybe you can bring some specialty toppings—you know, different flavored syrups and such."

"Whipped cream? Ice cream?"

She laughed. "Don't get carried away, Max," she said. "It's just breakfast."

"We'll make it memorable," he promised as he said good-bye.

He warned Marcie before she went to bed that evening, being careful not to break the news about the camping trip, but getting her excited about waffles and an early start. "That sounds great, Dad," she said as he tucked her into her bed. She leaned forward to give him a quick peck on the cheek and a tight hug.

Max smiled all over. "I'll have to come up with surprises more often if you're going to give me hugs like that."

"You can come to me any time you want a hug, Dad." To emphasize her point, she gave him another, squeezing harder and longer this time. "I've got lots more where those came from."

He chuckled, finding himself a little embarrassed by her easy affection, and more pleased than he could have said. "I'll remember that," he promised.

That night, he went to sleep already dreaming of a sweet little girl who loved him and a beautiful woman who might. *This camping trip is going to be the answer for all of us*, he assured himself as he slipped from daydreams into real ones.

* * *

So where's Logan Redhorse when I need him? Max asked himself wryly. He'd had the help of the guy at the wrecking yard to get the new engine into the back of Chris's truck, but Chris had been involved in state-required testing at the hog farm and had been unable to help him unload. Without the help of Logan's winch, he didn't know how he'd manage to wrestle the heavy motor onto the workbench.

"Looks like you could use a little help." D. J. walked up beside him, wiping grease off his hands with a heavy paper towel.

"I'd be grateful, man." Max eagerly took the hand D. J. proffered. "I don't know how I'll manhandle the thing by myself."

"It'll be tough enough for the two of us, I reckon." D. J. seemed to size up the job as he spoke. "If you want to grab hold right here . . ." He gestured where he thought Max could get a good purchase, "then I'll get 'round this side, like this. Ready?"

Max hadn't expected to be moving so quickly. "Sure," he said, taking a deep breath and feeling his muscles bunch as he bent his knees and prepared to take the weight. "On three?"

"Got it., One, two . . ."

"Three," Max said with him as both men lifted, taking the weight of the heavy engine. They swung it toward the workbench, then had to lift higher before they could put the motor into place. As Max wiggled the engine into a more secure position, he gasped a deep breath. "Thanks, man. Couldn't have done it without you."

"No problem," D. J. answered.

"I owe you one. How about you take a little break and I'll buy you a tall, cool one?"

D. J. ducked his head. "No thanks, man. I mean, I appreciate the thought and all, but—"

"Don't want to leave work early?" Max ventured. "I'll buy you a beer after you're ready to get off if you like."

"It's not that." Max thought D. J. looked uncomfortable, embarrassed almost. "It's just . . ." He turned to look Max squarely in the eye. "I'm an alcoholic. Haven't touched a beer in nearly eight months now, and I can't. Not ever again. Not if I don't want to go back to being a roaring drunk."

Now it was Max's turn to feel embarrassed. "Hey, I'm sorry. I had no idea. I never would have suggested—"

"It's okay. I know you didn't know. But hey, if you're willing to share a soda with me, I've got a couple in the cooler."

"Sure," Max said, "but I oughta be the one buying."

"You can bring me a new six-pack next time you come in if you like." He grinned. "I'm especially partial to orange and grape."

"I'll bring you a pack of each," Max promised as they opened the cooler and popped the lids on a couple of cans. As they rested against the workbench, sipping their sodas, Max probed a little. "That's quite an accomplishment, you know. Being sober for eight months, I mean. Lots of guy never get that far."

"I just wish I'd done it lots sooner," D. J. said. The regret was clear in his eyes and voice. "I lost a great woman and a couple of fine kids because of the booze. Course, I still see the kids, but it isn't the same."

"I know what you mean," Max said, thinking of how he had hardly known Marcie until this last few weeks.

"You, too?" D. J. asked.

Max shook his head. "Not the booze, no. I was more of a workaholic. When things got complicated at home, I just didn't go home. I was building a new company, and there was always the excuse of something that needed to be done at work."

"Yeah, I've seen that, too," D. J. answered, raising his can of grape soda in a mock salute. "To guys who don't wise up until it's too late."

Max nodded. "To divorced men who wish they'd known better."

"Hear, hear." D. J. touched his soda to Max's before swigging down another great draught. "So are you still spending long hours in the office? Or have you found somebody worth coming home to?"

"Don't know," Max answered honestly. "There's a woman here I've been seeing, a wonderful woman. Beautiful, smart, with a couple of great kids. I've been thinking about it. You?"

"Me, too. Name's Nancy. Met her at an A.A. meeting. She's recovering, too, sober more than a year now."

"Good for her." Max raised his can again and D. J. nodded approval. "Hope it works for you."

"Yeah, man. You, too."

"Thanks. I'm going to take her camping next week, over to the Grand Canyon. I think I'll propose to her there." Max didn't mention he'd already tried that once, and had blown it something awful.

D. J. looked like he was about to choke. He stared at Max, his eyes bugging. "You're going where?"

"The Grand Canyon," Max answered, confused. "Why?"

"My wife—that is, my ex-wife—and my kids are going camping at the Grand Canyon next week."

"That seems a strange coinci—" Max dropped his soda can, gasping. "Omigosh! You're Danny Sherwood!"

"And you're the Orange County hotshot who's been dating Cretia."

For a long, tense moment, the two men stood, sizing each other up. Max was running a mental list of the things he'd sworn he'd do to Danny Sherwood if he ever met the man.

He saw the same emotions reflected on "D. J.'s" face and knew he must have been thinking something similar. Danny took one slow step away, then quietly spoke. "I always figured if I ever met this guy my kids kept talking about, I'd rip him limb from limb."

Max kept his voice equally calm. "I always figured the same thing about meeting you."

There was another long silence, then Danny said, "It doesn't feel like I thought it would. I mean—heck, Max, you're kind of a nice guy."

Max slowly smiled. "I know what you mean," he said. "So are you."

"Never would have imagined it." Danny shook his head.

"Me, either." Slowly, Max reached forward, offering his hand.

Danny shook it, then the two clasped one another on the shoulder. "You marry her if you can, Max," Danny said, emphasizing each word, "but don't hurt her. She's a good woman. Me an' the booze have given her enough of a hard time."

Max felt his throat constricting. "You got it, buddy. I'll take good care of her, or if I can't, I'll fly out of here and leave her alone."

"I 'spect it's too late for that," Danny said. "You take good care of her, Max. Take good care of 'em all."

"I will," Max promised somberly.

"You're sure it'll be okay?" Cretia needed every modicum of reassurance Meg could offer her.

"I'm sure," Meg said. "Max helped me do a shakedown of all our camping equipment before we left last weekend. He knows how to set up everything, how to light the stove and the lantern, even how to use the cigarette lighter in the car to blow up the air mattresses so you don't have to hyperventilate to get comfortable. He's going to be an excellent camper.''

Cretia responded with a grimace.

''And the Grand Canyon is always beautiful,'' Meg went on. Cretia was almost sorry she'd gotten her started. ''This time of year the weather should be especially nice.''

''No rain?'' Cretia wrinkled her brow.

''Actually, a little afternoon shower is common this time of year, but they almost always blow over even faster than they blow up, and they leave the sky so clean and fresh-smelling, and full of beautiful sunsets.''

Cretia pursed her lips. ''You sound like a travel brochure.''

''I love camping. I wanted to be sure to start Alexis early.''

Cretia felt her eyes widen. ''You took Allie with you?''

''Of course,'' Meg said, ''and she did just great. We took a little inflatable swimming pool—a small one, just three feet across—and it made a perfect bed. She couldn't roll out of it, and it kept her nice and warm. She couldn't have been more snug in her own little bed.''

''You took Allie with you.'' Cretia was still amazed.

''Honest,'' Meg insisted, ''you're going to have a great time. And it's about time you took a break.''

''Oh, you know I have. Why, just last week—''

''That was comp time to keep me from having to pay you time-and-a-half. That's different from real vacation time, and you know it.''

Cretia allowed herself a small smile. ''Okay, you have a point. But you need to know that I'd never leave you in the lurch around here. You can't imagine how much I appreciate this job, Meg, and everything you and Kurt have done for me—''

''We haven't done a thing you didn't earn with hard work and lots of talent,'' Meg assured her. ''You know I had my doubts when you first applied for the receptionist's job, but you've won your way with all of us. Both Kurt and I are glad to have you in the office.'' She dropped her voice in a more suggestive tone. ''We'd enjoy having you in the family, too.''

''I—'' Cretia sat blushing, her mouth half-open.

''You don't have to say anything,'' Meg said. ''We can all see the way Max looks at you. And frankly, you have the same expression when you look at him. You make a good couple, and the kids seem to get along—''

''Yes, they do,'' Cretia answered, finally finding her voice, ''but Meg—''

''Don't worry about us,'' Meg assured her. ''If the time comes when you want to pack up and move to Orange County, Kurt and I will understand. We'll find it impossible to replace you, but we'll understand.''

Cretia shook her head. ''I'm not going to be packing up or moving anywhere, Meg. You two have given me so much—''

Meg laughed. ''Don't be silly, Cretia. If you get a chance to make a life with someone you love, don't let this place stand in the way. You're very good at what you do here, but it *is* just a job.''

''Not to me, it's not.'' Cretia felt her throat tightening.

''Really, Cretia—''

Lucretia Gina Vanetti Sherwood brushed away tears. ''Now, where's that invoice for those folks in Michigan? I had it here just a second ago.''

''Cretia—''

''Please, Meg. I can't talk about this right now.''

''Okay, but if you ever—''

''Please?''

Meg gave her a pleading look, then slowly shook her head. ''All right. We'll do this your way. For now, anyway.''

"Thanks. I appreciate that." Cretia sat down at her desk and turned her attention to her paperwork, but a long several minutes passed before her eyes stopped swimming and she was able to focus again.

"Wow!" Danny said as he leaned over the rail, staring down into the Grand Canyon. "Wow!"

Max chuckled, easing Danny away from the precipice. "It is something of a 'wow,' isn't it?"

Cretia shook her head. "I've seen thousands of pictures, even video. Nothing gives you the same sense you get from standing here, just looking at the immensity of it."

Max nodded. "I know what you mean."

They stood there, the five of them, posed in reverential silence, giving Nature its due.

They had arrived just a little after noon, found their campsite quickly, and taken only a few minutes to unload the car. Max still needed to set up their camp, but he had thought it wise to start everyone off with the high-quality view from the south rim. Maybe once they saw the canyon, they'd be more eager to pitch in on the duller tasks.

Apparently it worked. When he asked for their help a few minutes later, the whole group cooperated, moving back to the campsite to help with setup. They'd been equally cooperative, if more than a little shocked, when he had informed them of his meeting with Danny Sherwood. Even that had gone better than he could have hoped, though Cretia had shaken her head in wonder. Of course, he hadn't told her he had her ex-husband's blessing to marry her. *This is a charmed trip*, Max thought to himself, feeling rather smug. *I was right; it's going to be great for us all.*

The sensation stayed with him as the tents went up easily, the air mattresses all held firm, and Cretia even commented on the "comfortable bed" he had created for her in the two-room cabin tent that was now known as the Girls' Place. The smaller, two-man structure they called the Guys' Place was more than roomy enough for Max to share with Danny. Within an hour, the entire camp was set up, the coolers filled with ice, and the sleeping bags rolled out, ready for occupancy.

Max congratulated himself on the careful planning he and Cretia had done together this past week. They had food for every meal, and a full first aid kit, just in case. Everyone was looking forward to the beginning that evening of their planned Rook tournament—Cretia and her daughter against Max and his, with Danny keeping score. And they'd brought some table games, a small stack of entertaining books to read, and extra batteries for Max's CD player, so they'd always have music when they wanted it. They'd even brought extra canteens and a couple of backpacks, in case they decided to hike into the canyon before their vacation ended. *We worked so well together, really well, just like a well-established couple*, Max thought, pleased with himself, as he put the canned food into place and closed the cupboard.

That's when Cretia approached, rubbing at a raw spot on her arm. "Do we have insect repellent?" she asked, "Because I think I need some."

"Insect repellent?" Max looked at her blankly. "I'll bet they have some in the store." How could he have forgotten insect repellent? As he made the short hike to the general store, he hoped insect repellent was the only thing he'd forgotten.

This needs to go well, he told himself as he walked. *Our future may depend on it*. That idea alone was enough to scare him into a cold sweat. *Are you sure this is what you want, Max?* he asked himself as he paid for the repellent and started his return hike. *Cretia's a fine woman, but so was Joanna, and you'd have three kids to disappoint now.*

Are you sure you're willing to try again? 'Course, if you back out now, you'll have to deal with D. J. He chuckled, then felt surprise as a quiet, abiding peace settled in the center of his chest, assuring him this was exactly what he wanted.

"Aw, but Mom, why not?" it was probably the sixth time that evening that Danny had asked the same question, in one way or another. "We'd only go down as far as Indian Gardens. You can practically see that from the top."

"Yeah, Mom," Lydia chimed in. "It's only four-point-six miles down the Bright Angel Trail—"

"And about twelve miles back," Cretia answered, laying down a green Three on the green Two Max had led. "I don't think you three are prepared for a hike like that, especially not in the canyon heat."

"We'd have plenty of water," Marcie contributed as she took the hand with her green Fourteen. "Dad brought good canteens, and Lydia and I could carry extras in the backpacks. We could take snacks, too—"

"To replenish our essential nutrients," Danny quoted from the hiking information the park handed out. "So we don't suffer water intoxication."

"Water intoxication." Cretia shook her head. "Who would have imagined there could be such a thing?"

"It does sound funny, doesn't it?" Marcie led the green Thirteen.

"It makes sense when you think about it," Max said. "If you're sweating out a quart an hour—"

"Another good reason why I don't think the kids should hike down there," Cretia interrupted, laying down the green Four.

"—and you're getting plenty of water, but not replacing the sugars and salts, you can end up thinning your blood to the point it will no longer sustain you," Max finished, then saw the you're-not-helping-me-here look Cretia threw him. "At least, that's what the park's literature says." He tried to help his partner accrue points by laying down the green Ten.

"And it's only one of the hazards," Cretia continued as Lydia played the Rook, taking the hand. She paused for the requisite round of moans from Max and Marcie and gloating by Lydia. "There are at least three different kinds of poisonous snakes down there, not to mention scorpions and a variety of poisonous plants—"

"And those cute little Kaibab squirrels with the pointy ear tufts," Lydia said in a mocking tone. She led the black One. "Really, Mom, there are snakes and stuff at home in Rainbow Rock, but we've never encountered any of them. There's no reason to think we will here, either."

"It looks pretty dangerous to me," Cretia said.

Marcie was going for the divide-and-conquer strategy. "What do you think, Dad? You said you planned for us to do some hiking while we're here, and we're going home day after tomorrow. We've seen everything there is to see from the rim. If we want to go down into the canyon at all, tomorrow should be the day, don't you think?"

Max looked nervously at Cretia. "The ranger did say the hike to Indian Gardens and back was fairly light," he said. "He said people in good physical condition could easily make it down and back in a few hours."

"And we'd start first thing in the morning," Lydia wheedled. No one seemed to notice the game had stalled.

"The ranger said the biggest hazards occur with older people in poor condition, or folks who don't take enough food and water, or those who start too late in the day," Marcie said. "We're all young and tough, we'll carry plenty of water and enough trail snacks to get by, and we can start shortly after dawn, before it even gets hot."

"We'll stay together, too," Lydia added, then, turning to her brother, "won't we, Danny?"

"Yeah, sure," he answered helpfully. "We'll stay together all the way."

"Promise?" Cretia asked, and the girls signaled in triumph over her head.

"Promise," Danny said, solemnly crossing his heart. "Even if Lydia's a pain."

"Yeah, like I'm gonna be the one who's a pain," Lydia grumbled.

Cretia flashed her a worried look. "You can't even get along here in the campsite with Max and me watching," she said. "How can you handle the trail where you'll be on your own?"

"It's a real clear, easy trail, Mom," Lydia persisted. "And you know I get along just fine with Danny when I have to." She made a face at her brother, who responded with an even uglier one.

Cretia sighed. "Max, are you sure they'll be okay?"

Max felt an odd little shiver go down his spine, but he quieted it. "They'll be fine," he said, taking Cretia's hand. "They're good kids, strong and fit. They bicker and tease, but they hang together when they need to. The path *is* clear and well marked, at least as far as Indian Gardens, and it really shouldn't take them more than a few hours both ways." He paused, gently stroking her hand. "They're going to be fine, Cretia. Let them go."

She sighed, and Max knew they'd won. "Okay, but you have to follow through with that early start," she said to the kids. "If you're still sleeping at ten in the morning like you were yesterday and today, there's no way I'm going to let you go."

"We won't be sleeping," Lydia promised.

"Or even if you're still in camp bickering and complain-

ing about who has to carry the most water,'' Cretia continued. ''You're gone by nine or you don't go. Understood?''

''Understood,'' Lydia answered, with Danny echoing
close behind her.

''You won't be sorry,'' Marcie assured her. ''We're
gonna have a great hike.''

''Just make sure it's safe.'' Cretia blinked, then seemed
to remember the cards. ''Who led?''

Lydia spoke up. ''I did, Mom.''

''Then it's your play, Marcie,'' Cretia said, focusing on
her cards and rubbing at the crease that had formed between
her eyebrows. Marcie dutifully laid down the black Three.

''It's going to be okay, Cretia. Really it is,'' Max assured
her. He paused to take her hand and smile into her eyes
before turning back to the game, laying down points with
the black Ten.

''I hope so,'' Cretia mumbled.

''I'm glad you let them go.'' Max slid his arm around
Cretia, drawing her close as they turned from the canyon
rim where it overlooked the Bright Angel Trail. True to
their word, the kids had been up and ready to go before
eight-thirty. He and Cretia had watched them start their
hike, waving until they were ant-size spots on the canyon
floor, well on their way to the green oasis known as Indian
Gardens. ''They're going to have a great time.'' He reached
up to smooth the wrinkle in her brow. ''And they're going
to be just fine. Honest.''

She smiled. ''I think they probably are, but I'm entitled
to worry if I want. I'm a mother, after all.''

''Yes, you are,'' he answered, ''and a good one. Which
brings me to the real reason I wanted the kids to go hiking
today.''

''And that is?''

"Since you're such a fine mother and all, how'd you like to be Marcie's new stepmother?"

Cretia sighed, shaking her head. "Max Carmody, you do have the most romantic ways of proposing."

"I'm not proposing," he answered simply. "Not yet." Then he dropped to one knee in the middle of the road, within full sight of several groups of curious tourists, taking her hand in both of his. "*Now* I'm proposing."

Cretia stifled a nervous giggle. "For heaven's sake, Max. Get up. Everyone's watching."

"I'm in love with you, Cretia, and I don't care who knows it." Max leaned forward, reverently kissing her hand. "Cretia, will you marry me?"

All around them people stopped to watch. Cretia blushed, dropping her voice. "Get up, Max. *Please.*"

"But you didn't answer my question. Will you marry me, Cretia?"

"Max, get up right now. Hurry, while we can still get out of here with some dignity."

"Too late," he said, smirking at her. "So you'd better answer me, or—"

"All right, all right!" She couldn't help laughing. "Yes, Max, I'll marry you."

Max whooped and jumped to his feet, then threw both arms in the air. "She said yes!" he announced to the fifty-or-so tourists who all applauded while Cretia groaned and hid her face. "There now," he said. "Mission accomplished. We can walk back to the campsite."

"I'm glad I'll never have to face any of these people again," Cretia grumbled as they walked away, arm in arm, applause still sounding behind them.

"Why?" Max said, happier than he'd ever been in his life. "They're happy for us. We should be happy for us, too."

"I am," she said. "Max, when shall we tell the kids?"

"How about next week?" he suggested. "Monday is my birthday."

"Really? I never thought to ask about your birthday. Monday, is it?"

"Monday, August fourth," he answered. "We can take the kids to dinner and tell them then."

"Only if you let me buy," she said. "I won't have you buying your own birthday dinner. Better yet, let me cook for you at my place. My boss is a slave driver, but I think if I ask nicely, she'll let me go a little early. Uh, how many candles on that birthday cake?"

"What a subtle way to get around to that delicate subject. You first. Just looking at you, I'd guess you were under thirty, but I know you had Lydia when you were almost ready to graduate from high school."

"I'm thirty-one," she answered evenly. "I turned thirty-one last tax day, April fifteenth, and I swear I've earned every year of it."

Max clucked his tongue. "Still practically a child," he said. "Now I feel like a cradle robber. A sweet young thing like you isn't going to want an old duffer like me when you find out I'm turning forty next week."

"Forty?" She looked incredulous.

"Forty. The big Four-O."

She gave him a look of mock suspicion. "So you're looking for somebody who can take care of you in your old age, right?"

"You wicked, wicked woman." He kissed her, full on the mouth and still in view of a number of tourists, some of whom cheered again as they watched. "Does that feel like the work of an old man?"

"Hardly," Cretia answered, breathless. They walked on for a short way, then she said, "Max, there are some things we still need to talk about."

"I know. All those practical matters you didn't want to discuss before."

"I wasn't adverse to a discussion. I just wanted the romance first."

"Oh, so now I've filled the romance requirement, we can talk?"

"Um-hmm." She'd never looked so beautiful.

He decided to say it. "You know you are the most beautiful woman in the world, don't you?"

She blushed again, color rising in her cheeks. "No, but I'm glad if you think so."

"I know so," Max said, confident. "So, about those other things we need to talk about. I think I have everything figured out."

"That's exactly what we need to talk about," Cretia said as they reached their campsite. "Sit down, Max. We have some serious talking to do."

His stomach sinking, Max sat.

Chapter Nine

Cretia waited for Max to settle on the picnic bench in their campsite before she began to speak, dreading the confrontation their circumstances had created. "Before I say anything else, Max, I want you to know that I love you and I would like to marry you. Still, I wish you hadn't forced the issue when you proposed in front of all those people."

Max looked thoughtful. "I don't think I like the sound of that."

Cretia realized she was pacing. She sat next to Max. "There are things we should have talked about, should have worked out, before we make commitments."

"I think the commitments are already made," Max said meaningfully.

Cretia didn't want to see him hurt or angry, but there were details they would have to work out sooner or later, and sooner seemed wiser if they wanted this to last. "For instance, have you thought about where we'd live?"

"As a matter of fact, I have. I was looking around my little two-bedroom condo when I was back there a couple of weeks ago. Clearly it's a bachelor's kind of place—

162

sterile, and too small for all of us. I figure we'll need to go house-hunting when—"

"Not in Orange County, Max."

He paused. "What? You like L.A. better? Or would you rather head south, toward Mission Viejo and San Juan Capistrano?"

She swallowed. "Not in California, Max. I don't want to leave my job."

He seemed confused for a moment, then he grinned. "I get it now. I should have cleared that up in the first place." He stood, taking her hands in his. "You won't have to work anymore, sweetheart. When it comes to this sort of thing, I'm an old-fashioned guy, and I'm certainly capable of taking care of my wife, of my whole family, for that matter. As far as I'm concerned, you can quit your job tomorrow." He shrugged, giving her a boyish smile. "So you see, that one was easy. It's all taken care of."

Cretia gritted her teeth, and straightened her spine. "You don't understand, Max. This isn't about whether you can provide for us or not. I don't *want* to quit my job."

He dropped his hands and stepped back, staring at her as if she'd just sprouted horns. "Could you say that again?"

"I don't want to quit my job, Max. It means too much to me."

Anger transformed Max's features. "You're telling me you won't marry me because you'd have to give up your *job*?"

She tried to keep her voice calm. "I'm not saying that at all. I just want to work things out so I can continue the work I'm doing."

"Why? Didn't you hear what I just told you? You don't have to work."

"But I want to, Max." She took his hands, trying to help him see her side. "You don't understand what this job means to me. But try for a minute. Just imagine our situations were reversed, and I was telling you to give up your company and I'd take care of you and Marcie from now on. Do you see what that would mean to you?''

"But it isn't the same thing at all," Max protested.

"Why isn't it? Because I'm a woman?"

"Well, yeah—at least partly. That is the traditional pattern, isn't it? The woman tends the hearth and the man brings home the bacon."

Cretia forced herself to avoid a biting tone. "I've never known you to be chauvinistic or unfair before, Max. Besides, the traditional pattern involves people in their twenties who have children together, rather than raising each other's kids from previous marriages. We're hardly the people to exemplify tradition."

"Touché." He ran his hand through his hair. "But even then, you've got to see that there's a difference. I mean, really, Cretia. You surely can't look at my fifteen-year-old company that I've built from scratch, that employs more than two hundred people full-time and has a nationwide reputation in its field, then compare it with your little clerical job."

Cretia felt the angry flush color her features. "My little *what*?"

"Come on, Cretia. I don't mean to insult you, but be realistic. It's not like the work you do there is any big deal—"

Cretia's voice dropped low. She allowed it to carry some of the raw anger that suddenly pulsed through her. "I think you'd better stop now, Max, before you say something I won't be able to forget."

He threw his hands in the air. "Oh, come on! I mean, be real about this." He reached to catch her by the shoulders.

She pulled away. "Max, didn't you just tell me you love me?"

"Yes. I did, and I do. What's that got to do—"

Cretia interrupted, her voice breaking with emotion. "How can you say you love me when you obviously have so little respect for me?"

His eyes widened. He couldn't have looked more stunned if she'd poleaxed him. "Respect? Cretia, this isn't a question of respect. I have the utmost respect for you—"

"But not for what I do?"

"What 'what you do'? Cretia, you're making me crazy here! You want to answer a few phones, fill a few orders now and then? Great! Come on down to the auto parts factory and let me put you to work. You can even choose your own hours, work whenever—"

"Why, you arrogant snob! How *dare* you?" Her hand itched to slap him as anger tightened her throat. She couldn't remember the last time she'd been so furious, or hurt. "I'm a producer, Max, a full-fledged producer. Maybe you don't understand what that means, but there's a lot of responsibility involved, and it feels good to handle it well.

"I set up shoots and interviews, run quality control on sound and lighting, manage hundreds of little details that make all the difference in the world about the quality of the final product. And we're doing quality work here, Max. The earlier program that Meg and Kurt and Alexa made on this same subject was named the best documentary of the year. Best of the *year*, Max. In *Hollywood*. We have the chance to do that again with this program, and I can be a part of that. I, little Lucretia Sherwood, who had to struggle just to finish high school. I'm a producer for a prize-winning production company. And you have no right to dismiss that as if it's just—"

"Okay, okay, so it's more than answering phones.

You're a producer, all right? And you're right. I didn't realize how much goes into it. Still, you can't expect me to give up my company just for that.''

Cretia's heart ached. Tears were beginning to spill, but they were no longer merely angry. Now they were filled with sorrow, too. "Stop, Max. Just stop. I don't think I want to hear anything more from you today.'' She turned, stalking toward the Girls' Place.

He caught her arm. "You're ending it? Just like that?''

"Leave me alone, Max,'' she said with all the force she could muster. She brushed his hand away and entered the tent, zipping the door closed.

"Cretia, come out here and talk to me. Cretia, come out right now!'' For the next several minutes he stalked and spewed and sputtered, but Cretia didn't respond, and Max didn't violate the barrier of her zipped tent closure. Finally she heard him striding away, still muttering angry words under his breath. Cretia sat alone on her air mattress and bedroll, desultory tears streaming down her cheeks.

Max stalked and sputtered, muttering to himself, hiking from one canyon view to the next, punishing himself with harder and steeper hikes. He glanced at his watch. "Nearly noon,'' he said aloud. As near as he could figure it, it had been roughly three hours since Cretia had lost her mind. *What on earth is the matter with that woman?* he asked himself, pacing again. *Is she completely off her rocker? Or am I missing something here?* He carefully reviewed everything she had said, then everything he had said. *Nope, I'm not missing anything. She's lost it and that's all there is to it. Either that, or she doesn't really love me and needs an excuse to break it off.* As soon as he thought that, he shook his head, forcing the thought away. Angry as he was, he didn't really believe that. He couldn't afford to. Cretia loved him just as he loved her. *So why is she being so stubborn about this? I don't get it. I just don't get it at all.*

Maybe that's the problem. It was that second little voice, speaking from his inner self, or his conscience, or wherever. *Maybe you don't understand what she's trying to say to you. Maybe you should listen harder.*

Oh, brother, he answered the little voice. *That just goes to show how much* you *know.* Then, because he couldn't think of any better option, he started back for the campsite.

He found it in total disarray—sleeping bags rolled and stacked on the picnic table, air mattresses deflated and piled on a camp chair, supplies gathered and boxed. Cretia was in the process of knocking down the women's tent. Her eyes were swollen and her face flushed. She looked so miserable he wanted to hold and comfort her, and so furious he wanted to turn and get out of there quickly, before she flayed him alive.

Somewhat to his chagrin, the first thing out of his mouth was, "What on earth are you doing?"

She tossed him a look designed to melt glass. "As if that isn't obvious."

"But we agreed. We're leaving tomorrow."

"We agreed," she said pointedly, "that if I was miserable camping you'd take me home—and tell the kids it was all your idea." She looked at her watch and Max automatically glanced at his. Almost one. "I figure they'll be back in another hour, two at the most," she said. "You can tell them then." She pulled on a tent pole and the structure collapsed with a whoosh. Max felt the same sensation in his lungs.

"Listen, Cretia, I'm not sure if I know what happened here a while ago, but surely it doesn't have to ruin our vacation plans, or our future. We can work things out."

She put up a hand. "Not now, Max. I'm so hurt and

angry I don't even think I can talk to you now. I just want to go home.''

"Cretia, please—"

"Leave again if you want to. I can handle this by myself." He thought it sounded more like an order than an offer.

"But—" Her wounded, frozen expression stopped him cold. Aware that argument would serve no purpose, he let out a long, aggrieved sigh, and started taking down the tent he had shared with Danny. As he worked, he calculated. If the kids were back by three—and he could think of no reason at all why they shouldn't be—they could still be home by dinnertime. Maybe he could talk Cretia into going out with him and they could spend the evening talking, working things out.

Yeah, right, said his little voice. *She isn't talking to you here, where you're alone together in a peaceful, even romantic, environment. What makes you think she's going to want to talk to you when you get her back home, where all the problems are?*

Oh, shut up, he grumbled to the little voice. *Who asked you, anyway?*

Cretia stood on the south rim, overlooking the trailhead for the Bright Angel Trail. Below she could see the green oasis that marked the beginning of Indian Gardens. Most of the trail between her and the green was clearly visible, and the kids were nowhere in sight. "It's four o'clock," she said aloud. "They should be here by now."

"I'd have thought so, too."

She whipped around to see Max approaching behind her. "I didn't know you were here."

"I followed you down from the campsite."

"Oh."

Cretia turned and put her hands on the railing, staring

down at the trail. A family was strolling down the first hundred yards or so—a young father, his wife, and three children, two girls and a little boy, barely toddler size. Their happiness hurt her. She turned her eyes farther down the trail. A couple in denim shorts and camp shirts and wide straw hats hiked toward them, maybe a mile away. Their struggle suggested the steepness of the climb. She saw no one else on the trail, but everywhere she saw reminders that both trail hiking and family life could be challenging. She didn't need that reminder now, not with her children more than an hour late, not with Max standing beside her, silent as a morgue. She started to speak, to tell him she was going to talk to the rangers. He spoke up before she got the chance.

"I think I'll walk over to headquarters, see if there's someone there who knows how long the hike to Indian Gardens and back should take."

She nodded. Better for Max to go. Then she could stand here, watching for her children. For Marcie, too. "Okay." She didn't look up, but she noticed that he hesitated as he walked behind her. For a moment she thought he would touch her. He didn't, but walked on toward the park offices. She couldn't have said whether she was glad or disappointed.

You're going to have to deal with this, you know, her inner voice spoke. *You're going to have to talk with him, to try to help him understand where you're coming from.*

Yeah, I know, she answered her voice. *But I tried. You heard me try. I had no idea he'd be so stubborn, so unwilling to hear anything I had to say. Who'd have guessed sweet Max Carmody would turn out to be such a male chauvinist? And so insulting!*

Her pride still hurt, stung by his comments about her "little clerical job." The nerve of the man!

But he doesn't understand, Cretia. You know he doesn't.

It was that blasted inner voice again. For a moment she wondered if she wasn't better off without a conscience, or whatever that was. *He's never struggled the way you've had to, and it's tough for a man to see a woman's perspective. After all, he's never been there. Give the guy a break. . . .*

"Yeah? On which leg?" she mumbled aloud, angry with that part of her that was willing to hear, even when she was so clearly in the right and he was being so self-centered, so muleheaded, so . . .

An image popped into her mind, a memory of Angelica DeForest at Chris and Sarah's wedding, dropping out of view behind the piano while the audience applauded her music. *You were wrong about her,* her voice said. *For years you assumed she was being self-centered and arrogant. You were wrong about poor, shy Angelica. You could be just as wrong about Max.*

Okay, okay, she answered. *I'll talk to him. When the kids get back safely and we're home again, I'll give him another chance.* She conveniently ignored the idea that maybe she'd been putting him off on purpose, that the things she had to say would be tough on her self-esteem, that maybe she feared he wouldn't want her if he knew everything.

Instead she turned her attention to the trail. There was still no sign of the kids. The young family was turning back, the little boy in tears, the mother looking stressed and unhappy. Cretia turned away, unable to watch their distress. Just now, she was dealing with enough of her own.

Even as she thought it, Max came into view. "Well," he said, and the smile he gave her was a little too bright, a little too trying-to-be-brave. It frightened her. "There's good news and bad news."

She swallowed. "Go on."

"The good news is, there's a guy in there who just came

up the trail. He probably arrived no more than twenty minutes ago.''

''Khaki clothes and a safari hat?'' Cretia asked.

''Yeah. That's the one.''

''I saw him come in just as I arrived. You're right; it's only been a few minutes.''

Max nodded. ''He recognized my description of the kids and he said they were just getting into Indian Gardens when he was getting ready to leave there. He figures they'd want to rest a while before they started the hike up.''

''But they're not on the trail.''

''Not that we can see,'' Max corrected gently. ''The guy in the safari hat says there are lots of little bends and dips that aren't obvious from here, lots of places where he lost sight of the top as he was coming up. He figures they're probably on the trail back and we just can't see them yet.''

Cretia felt the first sense of relief she'd experienced this afternoon. ''That makes sense. Okay, so the bad news?''

Max looked somber. ''If there is a problem, we could be on our own—at least for a while.''

The fear was back. ''On our own? What does that mean?''

''The rangers were sympathetic, but they say they get hundreds of reports of hikers who aren't back as soon as they were expected. It's so common, they hardly notice anymore. Unless there's a confirmed report of an actual injury or a party has been missing for at least twenty-four hours, they can't spare people to help us. Even then, they can't offer much help. That's why there are all of those 'hike at your own risk' signs.''

Cretia's heart sank. ''Oh. But these are kids, Max, *young* kids. Danny's barely eleven, and the girls are only thirteen.''

''Shh, love, shh.'' Max stepped close, putting his arm around her in a gesture of mutual comfort. ''I made the same argument with the rangers and they eased up a bit. If the kids aren't back by the time it's fully dark, they'll lend me one of their summer workers to hike the trail with me.'' He drew her closer. ''Don't worry too much, love. It'll be all right.''

Some of Cretia's anger toward Max had already been consumed in her growing fear for their children. Relenting, she let him comfort her. After a moment, he said, ''Well, we aren't accomplishing much standing here.''

''What do you think we should do?'' she asked.

''If that guy is right and they're really on their way back, they'll be here in the next hour. Ninety minutes, maybe.'' Max looked at his watch, then at the sun, now low in the sky. ''Let's walk over to the camp store. I'll buy you a cold drink and we can meander back to the campsite. While we're waiting, I'll load up a backpack with lots of extra water, some food, some basic first aid—''

Cretia drew in her breath as he said that. Her gasp elicited a tight, sympathetic smile from Max.

''—just in case, Cretia. Just in case.'' He paused, turning toward the camp store. They began the walk together. ''If they aren't back by five-thirty, we'll bring the pack to the trailhead. If we can't see them from here by then, I'll start after them.''

''Darkness falls by eight,'' she reminded, suddenly fearing for him, too. ''But you're not going to wait for the ranger?''

''No. I guess there's too much dad in me now. I'll take one of the big lights, and a couple of extra flashlights in my pack.''

''You'd better pack some light blankets as well.'' She flashed him that same tight, sympathetic smile. ''Just in case.''

''Right,'' he answered.

Minutes later, drinks in hand, they were on their way

back to the campsite. While Max unpacked gear from the back of Jim's double-cab pickup, Cretia made a list of everything she thought he might need, trying to remember to conserve on space so Max could carry it all. By five, they had come up with a pack that contained all the basics. If the kids were in trouble, Max would be ready to help them.

"Well, I guess that's it," he said, hoisting it to prove to himself that the pack was manageable. "We still have a few minutes to go before we start for the trailhead." He put the pack down and sat beside her on the bench seat of the site's picnic table.

"Max?" Cretia suddenly felt a great need to talk to him, and a great fear of it. Both were overwhelming her. This couldn't wait.

"What, babe?" He moved closer, gently holding her.

"I'm worried about our kids," she began.

"Me, too." He kissed her hair, a comforting gesture.

She drew away so she could look him in the eyes. "But I'm worried about us, too."

He swallowed hard, trying for a brave smile. That gesture said more than his words. "Me, too."

She smiled at him, though the smile wavered a bit. "I want to talk to you about my job, about what it means to me." He looked away, grunting some indistinguishable sounds. "Please, let me say this. Some of it is kind of hard to say."

That got his attention. The warm and generous part of Max that she had come to know so well, the Max she knew and trusted, was there for her now, offering support. "Okay," he said. "Go on."

She sighed as she began, looking toward a nearby pine tree, focusing on the antics of a small gray squirrel. "My parents weren't poor. Middle class, I guess you'd call them, but always by the skin of their teeth. Dad was a butcher and Mom didn't work, so although there was always enough, we didn't have much for extras.''

She glanced at Max, who nodded to let her know he was listening.

''Dad always made an issue of what everything cost, and he used that as a way of controlling us kids. I'm not even sure he realized he was doing it, but it sure bothered me.'' She paused with a sigh.

Max's brow had furrowed. ''Controlling? How?''

''Little things. 'Get that room cleaned up by dinnertime, or you won't get your allowance this week,' '' she quoted, mimicking her father's booming voice. '' 'The band trip is going to cost forty-five dollars? That's outrageous! You'll have to earn at least half of that yourself or you won't be able to go.' It was always the money with Dad.''

''Um,'' Max grunted. ''I see what you mean. By the way, when were you in a band?''

''High school,'' she said. ''The clarinet. I haven't played in a long time, though.''

''I'd like to hear it sometime.''

''No. You wouldn't. Believe me.'' She grinned. ''Anyway, you're changing the subject.''

''Right,'' he answered, settling in again.

The banter had eased her mood. She relaxed a little, leaning against him. ''Looking back, I think now that maybe I rushed into the relationship with my ex-husband just to get away from Dad and always having to watch my pennies and be accountable for everything I spent. If that's what I was doing, I sure blew it.'' She smiled wryly, looking at the squirrel rather than at Max. ''It was ever so much worse with Danny.''

She felt the bitterness rising in her throat as painful images flashed through her mind. ''There was so little money and we fought over anything I ever spent, even for basics like groceries. Once he chewed me out for buying two gallons of milk instead of one.'' She paused. ''And I never spent a penny on myself, not after the first time I got a haircut.'' She had to stop then, remembering that terrible fight. Max stroked her shoulder, offering his support as he quietly waited.

''I wasn't working then. I'd barely managed to struggle through the last few weeks of school after Lydia was born, and I had no job skills. I suppose I might have taken more business classes if I'd known the direction my life would take, but I was smart and teachers had put me on a college-prep track. Then too, I was naive enough that I believed if I got married, my husband would take care of me.''

''That's what should have happened,'' Max said.

''Maybe,'' she answered, then pointedly added, ''but it didn't. Danny felt that if he earned it, it was his to spend. For years I never bought a thing for myself that I didn't have to beg for first. Not even maternity clothes. Not even a lousy tube of lipstick! Sometimes I had to beg to get basics for the kids. Once Lydia went without shoes for a week because she'd outgrown her only pair and her dad wouldn't part with the money for another.''

Max winced. ''It must have been pretty bad.''

''That was only the start.'' Cretia let her voice harden with her mood. ''After I left him, things only got worse. I still had no job skills, and life with Danny had so diminished my sense of myself that I didn't have the confidence necessary to build any. So instead—'' She paused, then glanced at Max, biting at her lip. ''—instead, I started looking for another husband. I thought it was the only way I could survive and take care of my children.''

She looked at Max to gauge his reaction. He was watching her with a serious expression, but he didn't seem to realize what she was really telling him. She sighed. She would have to be plainer.

"I became sort of the talk about town, Max. I went after every single man I saw."

His eyes widened, but he still wasn't seeing. "I think you're being tough on yourself, baby. I'm sure it wasn't that—"

"Don't, Max. Don't diminish this. You can ask Meg if you don't believe me. I tried for Jim before she came to town. Later I went after Kurt—"

He was seeing now. She could tell from the way his face was reddening. "Kurt McAllister? The guy you work for?"

"You know another Kurt in Rainbow Rock? Of course Kurt McAllister. He was the one who finally put me in my place."

"He did *what*? How?" Max looked murderous.

"First he made it clear that he was in no way interested in me, so plainly even I had to see it. Then, when I turned my attentions on a friend of his, he came to me and told me what stereotype he felt I was becoming, the desperate divorcée pursuing every man who came along."

"He *said* that to you?" Max's voice was choked with anger.

She took his hands. "He did, Max, and it was the kindest thing anyone has ever done for me. He held up a mirror and made me look in it. It was difficult for me, but it worked because, along the way, he also told me he thought I was too smart for that, too capable. He said if I applied all the effort I was using to find a man to finding a job instead, I'd be able to take care of myself without a man." She touched his face. "Max, it was one of the most difficult conversations I've ever had with anyone, and one of the best. While Kurt was making me see myself as I had become, he was also giving me the confidence to become something else."

"You weren't furious?" Max stared at her in wonder.

"Of course I was. I was so hurt and angry, it was painful

to contain it. So I didn't. I lashed out, screaming at him. He took all my abuse, then he told me it was up to me whether I was going to keep going downhill or turn my life around and make something of myself. Later, when the anger had cooled a little, that was the part I remembered. And I believed him. I've always been grateful to him for that.''

Max seemed calmer now, thoughtful. He nodded. ''Go on.''

''I got my first job shortly after that, cleaning houses. It barely kept us alive, but I was used to living on very little. After that I kept improving my circumstances. With each new job, each raise I got, each compliment from my bosses, I gained more confidence. Then I used that confidence to learn more. By the time Alexa came to town, Meg and Kurt were looking for a receptionist in their office. Alexa was new and didn't know what my history with Kurt was, so when she bumped into me at the coin laundry, she told me about the job and I applied for it.''

Max's expression had changed. She thought she saw admiration in it. ''Whew. That must have taken some gumption.''

''Yeah, it did. But it was worth it. And Kurt, bless his soul, was willing to give me another chance. I started out just answering phones. As I proved I could handle a job, they'd teach me another.'' She broke into her own narrative, cutting to the chase. ''Are you beginning to see now, Max? I've thought about it a lot, more than I ever wanted to. I know you aren't like Danny—or my father, for that matter—and that you mean it when you say you'd like to take care of the kids and me. But I can't do that. I can't let go of this little bit of independence that I've worked so hard to win. It isn't just the job title or the money, either. It's the confidence in myself, the self-esteem, the way I feel about who I am. Please try to understand. I wouldn't be the same person as an Orange County housewife. I couldn't be.''

For a long moment, Max just looked into her eyes. Then he slowly leaned forward and kissed her, long and meaningfully. ''You've given me a lot to think about,'' he said.

She tried for a smile, but she didn't think it came out very well. There were too many tears in it. ''I was afraid if you heard all that, you wouldn't want me anymore.''

''Not want you? Oh, honey.'' He stood, pulling her into his arms, holding her against his chest as if he'd never let her go. ''Of course I want you.'' Then he held her away again, looking into her eyes. ''I love you, Cretia. I love your kids, too. And Marcie loves you all. I'm not sure how we're going to work things out, but we will. That much I'm sure of. Just now, however—'' He paused, looking at his watch. ''I think it's time I go find our kids.''

She blinked tears away, nodding, then reached for the backpack. ''Here,'' she said. ''Let me help you put this on.''

Max nodded and turned his mind toward the trail.

Chapter Ten

Max hiked, worrying harder as the trail grew darker. He'd been out for nearly an hour, and moving fast. The green of Indian Gardens lay before him, not far ahead. *I should have found the kids by now*, he mused, glancing at his watch. *Six-thirty already. What if they're not there? What if they're hurt? Something is surely wrong or they'd have been back before this*. He stopped the thoughts there, not wanting to see the images that were beginning to creep in around the edges.

Some hundred and fifty yards ahead of him, two hikers crested a rise and came within sight. He glanced their way, dismissed them, then quickly looked back as one called, "Max?" It was Lydia's voice.

"Lydia? Danny?" he asked, pumping his walk into a jog. "Where's Marcie?"

"Up ahead," Lydia called, running toward him. "In the cabin."

"Is she all right?"

"Yeah. She's fine."

They met in the middle then and he grabbed them both, hugging them roughly against him, dropping a kiss on

Lydia's forehead, rubbing Danny's hair in harsh affection. He couldn't remember when he'd been so glad to see anyone. Touching them now reminded him that it wasn't just Cretia he loved. He'd fallen for the whole family.

"I'm so glad you're safe," he said again. "So glad. Please, tell me about Marcie."

Quickly, in scattered bits and spurts, the kids filled him in. They had arrived at Indian Gardens before noon and had rested in the small wayside cabin there, a one-room shack of native stone, eating and drinking and gathering energy for the walk back.

"That's when Danny insisted on going farther down the trail," Lydia said.

"Danny!" Max turned to him. "You knew better than that."

"I just wanted to walk a little ways, just down through the rest of Indian Gardens in the green part."

"We told him not to, Dad." Lydia blushed. "I mean, Max. We reminded him what we'd promised, but he said he was going to go anyway, no matter what we said, so we decided we'd better stay together."

Max, overcome by her little slip, simply nodded. "I see. Go on."

"That's where I found the lady," Danny explained.

"What lady?"

As the kids went on, Max pieced the story together. They had come upon a middle-aged woman who was hiking with her teenaged daughter. The woman had apparently been overcome by heat and fatigue and lay resting by the path. Sympathetic to the daughter's fear, the kids had stayed with them, offering food, water, and encouragement, until the woman felt strong enough to make it to the cabin.

"It took us a long time to get her there, Dad," Lydia finished. This time she didn't even bother to correct herself. Max wasn't sure she realized what she'd said. "She's kind of a big lady, and it took all three of us girls, carrying her stuff and walking with her, to get her into that cabin. She's resting down there now with her daughter. We knew you and Mom would be worried, so Marcie said she'd stay with them while Danny and me came back to tell you guys what's going on here.''

"But you're both all right," Max said, reassuring himself, "and Marcie's all right."

"Yeah," Danny said. "It's just that lady who's in trouble."

"I'm so glad," Max said, hugging them both again. At that moment he resolved to do whatever he had to do to make these children and their mother his. "I'm proud of you," he said to them. "You've done the right thing, but you're right about your mom. She's really worried. So here's what I want you to do. Get a good drink of water, then head back up the trail. Here, you'll need these lights because it's getting dark." He gave them two of the smaller flashlights. "Pace yourselves and stop to nibble or get a drink whenever you need to, but keep up a good, quick pace and get there as soon as you can. Your mom will be waiting by the trailhead. Got it?"

They both nodded.

"When you get there, tell the rangers at headquarters that there's a middle-aged woman overcome by heat exhaustion in the rock cabin at Indian Gardens. Ask them to send help. Okay?"

"Got it," Lydia answered.

"Great," he said. "Go now, and good luck. I love you both."

"I love you, too," Lydia said, and punctuated it with a rough kiss on the cheek.

"Me, too," said Danny, hugging Max around the waist.

His eyes were moist as he hugged back, then sent them

on their way. "Tell your mom everything's going to be all right," he said.

"We will," they assured him.

He watched until they'd rounded the curve in the trail, out of his sight. They were making good time, and he knew how relieved Cretia would be to see them. Then he turned, on his way to find his own daughter and to make good his promise that everything would be all right.

"Daddy!" Marcella threw herself into his arms as soon as he stepped into the stone cabin. "How did you get here so fast?"

It took him a moment to clarify that part of the story, then he asked her, "Who are your friends?" and was roughly introduced to Tamara Snyder of Bend, Oregon, and her mother, Mrs. Snyder.

"Hi," he said, kneeling beside the pale woman who sat propped against one wall. "The kids tell me you've been having a hard time here."

"Um," the woman mumbled.

"Do you have a first name, Mrs. Snyder?" he asked as he checked her pulse in her wrist and shined his flashlight into her eyes. He wasn't a paramedic, but he recognized a solid if too-rapid pulse when he felt it, and he could tell when pupils were appropriately reactive.

"Lacey," she murmured.

He nodded. "Nice to meet you." Lacey Snyder wasn't in great shape, but she'd be fine, once she got back to the top and had a little time to rest and recuperate. He went back to the girls. "It looks like you've done very well here," he said, then reassured Tamara, "Your mom is going to be just fine."

"Oh, thank goodness!" the girl said, and began crying.

"Tell me about it," he said to Marcie.

"I think she had water intoxication, Dad," Marcie explained, listing all the symptoms. "It was just like they described in the brochures. We tried to get her to eat, but she kept mumbling that she didn't feel like eating anything. Finally, after we got her in here, we were able to get some food into her. She seemed to do better after that. She couldn't even tell us who she was when we first saw her, so she's doing lots better now."

"You did just great, Marcie." Max hugged his daughter gratefully against him, finally banishing the fear that had been growing all afternoon. "I can't tell you how proud I am."

During the next half-hour, they stayed with the Snyders, sharing their blankets when the temperature began to fall and encouraging Mrs. Snyder to take more food. By the time the paramedic arrived, Mrs. Snyder was doing much better. With a round of thanks, they found themselves free to go.

Max hefted his backpack as they left the cabin, and put an arm around his daughter. "Now we have a great moonlight hike to look forward to," he said. *Not to mention a long drive home and some pretty intense emotional stuff to deal with at the top*, he added in the privacy of his thoughts. *It's still going to be a long night.* He couldn't have been more grateful when he got to the top and found Cretia waiting with the unpacked truck. She drove them to the campsite where Lydia and Danny waited with a hot meal ready and the camp completely rebuilt, neatly set up with beds ready to crawl into. After the day they'd had, it was exactly what everybody needed.

Cretia awakened early and crawled out of her sleeping bag, heading toward the public rest rooms. She was surprised when she returned to the campsite to find Max standing near the picnic table, looking toward the east.

"It's going to be a beautiful sunrise," he said as she approached.

"It certainly is," she agreed, stepping close.

He put his arm around her. "Thanks again for what you and the kids did last night," he said. "It was so good to come back to warm food and a comfortable place to sleep."

"I thought that's what I'd want after a long hike," she said.

"You were right."

For a few moments, they paused, watching the sky grow lighter. It had reached a soft dove color. "This is the time of day the local Native American people call White Dawn," Cretia said.

"White Dawn," Max repeated. "Seems appropriate."

"There's a legend to go with it," she added. "Both the Hopi and the Navajo tell the story, though it's a little different for each. I like the Navajo story better."

When he didn't respond, she went on. "Seems in the early times of creation, Sun married Changing Woman, and lived with her in her hogan on one side of the world. Later, when her sister, Turquoise Woman, was lonely, Sun married her, too, and began a daily migration across the sky from the hogan of one wife to that of the other.

"Each day, as he left the hogan of Changing Woman to make his way across the sky, he would climb the ladder that led up out of the smoke hole in her hogan and he'd wrap himself in a gray fox fur until the day grew warmer. Then he'd put on the lighter yellow fox fur and bring the Yellow Dawn."

"That works," Max said, content to let her tell him anything if she'd just stay snuggled against him.

"Maybe that's what you need, Max," Cretia said, flashing him a teasing look.

"What? A gray fox fur?"

"No. Two wives. One here in Rainbow Rock, and the other at home in Orange County."

"No way," Max said vehemently. "You're all I want, Cretia. You and the kids are all I've ever need. And *this* is my home—at least, Rainbow Rock is, as long as you and our kids are out here."

She looked up, afraid to hope. "But how can we—"

"It's obvious. At least, it seemed obvious when it occurred to me about an hour ago. I was lying there unable to sleep—"

"You, too?"

"Mmm."

"In spite of that heavy hike?"

"Shh. Let me tell this," he said, gently kissing her quiet. "I was lying there worrying about us when it occurred to me that I can go on running Carmody Auto Parts the same way I have been all summer. The plant is more productive than it's ever been, and I've been turning out new parts at a faster rate than I ever have, even when I was starting the company.

"I talked with Nate, my production manager, when I was home . . ." He interrupted himself, grinning. "I mean, when I was in Orange County last month. He told me he thought I ought to stay away from the plant. I was insulted at first, but then I realized he was right. I've been planning to do that, too. I just always thought I'd stay away from it in Orange County. When I realized I could stay away from it anywhere . . . Well, I thought, why not here?"

"Then that's it? Just like that?"

"If you don't mind. We'll still have to look for a new house, though. You and the kids don't have room for Marcie and me."

"Marcie, too?" She asked, her face bright with hope.

"I haven't talked to her mother yet, but I think it's a good possibility." Max was smiling, and Cretia felt a deep peace seeping over her. "When I picked Marcie up after their last visit, Joanna said she'd never seen her happier. She said she thought Rainbow Rock had been good for Marcie."

"I hope she'll let her stay."

"So do I." He looked into her eyes. "So, one more time, Cretia, without any tourists watching, or the kids here, or anybody but just you and me. Marry me? Let me live with you and love you and learn to appreciate the work you do?"

She sighed and leaned against him. "I love you, Max. I have to be the person I've come to be, but I swear I'll try to be a good wife to you, too."

"The person you are is the only one I want," he assured her.

She reached toward him, standing on her tiptoes, and he wrapped his arms around her, taking all he could of the love and hope and commitment she was promising. When they finally parted, she sighed softly, then said, "So shall we tell the kids on your birthday, the way we planned?"

His eyes twinkled as he grinned at her. "Let's roll them out and tell them right now. We can celebrate the news for my birthday. We'll make it a combination birthday-engagement party."

She smiled. "I'll make a birthday cake with a bride and groom on top."

"And forty candles."

"Forty candles," she said gravely, her heart alive with joy. "That's one for every year I plan to live with you, Max Carmody—except for the last twenty or so."

He grinned, happier than he'd ever been. "Cretia, my love, I'm looking forward to them all."